DRAGON UNITY

Blood of the Ancients Book 12

DAN MICHAELSON

D.K. HOLMBERG

Copyright © 2023 by ASH Publishing

Cover art by Damonza.com

All rights reserved.

No part of this book may be reproduced in any form or by any electronic or mechanical means, including information storage and retrieval systems, without written permission from the author, except for the use of brief quotations in a book review.

Chapter One

SERENA

THE PALACE FELT DIFFERENT.

It had always been her home, and as she grew up, she felt its essence permeating the walls and filling the rooms. She connected with that essence, but now that she had raised to dragon soul and then subsequently to dragon blood, she felt the power in a very different manner.

Whatever Rob had done, which had 'forced the effect of the unity,' as he liked to call it, redirected some of the power there away from her mother and into Serena. She could feel it flowing out from the palace. It was connected to her; in a way, it felt like it was flowing for her and meant to be found by her.

She walked through the main corridor and paused, casting a worried glance at the entrance ahead.

Serena had never worried about the soldiers before, but ever since the palace had turned on her, she became far more concerned about what the soldiers might do and how they might react to her. Although lately, the soldiers have only been watching, as though they were waiting for her command. She could feel the energy of the soldiers and the way that it manifested, as though, a part of them simply existed for her.

They now stood guard inside the palace, no longer lining the walls.

She took a deep breath, letting it out slowly. Serena was late, and though she hated being late, the others were going to wait on her behalf, and Serena wasn't even going to feel bad about that.

"Where are you?"

The voice came from inside her mind, the dragon mind connection that bridged her and Griffin together.

"Am I making you wait too long?" she thought with a smile.

Griffin huffed.

"You know I don't care for this side of things."

Serena rolled her eyes, as she continued walking.

"You never cared for anything other than fighting uncle," she replied.

She imagined her uncle grunting at this point. She knew where he was, even if she didn't have the dragon mind linked to him. She could *feel* him.

When Rob forced the unity of essence, she became more aware of the power inside the palace and what she could do with it. She could feel the energy that existed, and her unique form of essence created ripples in the wave of energy that flowed through the palace. Those ripples allowed her to detect where they were, what they were doing, and, when she really focused, how they were using their essence.

She breathed out and hurried down the hallway until she reached the great hall where her uncle was waiting with the rest of the council. It was far too long for her to have been away, but she had been busy with other things. Not the least of which was dealing with her mother. And now they had to deal with the consequences of that. It was time for her to reveal the truth to her people, even though she had wanted to have a council and did not want to rule.

Something that Griffin said stuck with her. Even though she might not want to rule, some people might want it from her. A dragon queen has led those living there for as long as they can remember. The palace was a marker of power. This meant that Serena may have had to *choose* to lead, even if it was to defray some of that.

The door opened before her outstretched hands could grab the brass handles. A pair of soldiers dressed in maroon uniforms, with curved swords strapped to their waists, stood on either side with their heads bowed as they waited for her to enter. Once she stepped in, they marched alongside her.

Serena stopped and gestured for them to remain as they were while she continued to the table at the center of the room. Griffin was already seated, shaking his head as the soldiers returned to their position beside the doors. The others seated at the table were all at dragon-mind level, none having progressed any level higher than that. Griffin was the only dragon soul present.

Her father could have been here but chose not to attend, having been far more intrigued in returning to his research. He also felt as if he'd lost his place in the city, and no longer wanted to spend any time ruling, nor did he want to spend time around her mother. Serena didn't blame him for that and was perfectly content with their current arrangement.

"Thank you for giving us your time, Serena," Griffin said, getting to his feet and speaking aloud.

She could sense his amusement through his dragon soul connection to her. Ever since Griffin had raised to dragon soul, the connection he'd formed had changed into one that shared some aspect of emotion with her. Serena wondered if she had done the same thing to him.

She knew what she did to Rob, through the existing conduit, which also made her feel his emotion. Though these days, the emotion she felt from Rob was a bit more constrained, partly because he'd progressed to whatever he was now and had gained unimaginable power. Serena had seen him using that power, 'the unity of essences,' and knew that it was something impossible. He had *remade* his essence.

The simple idea was so hard for her to fathom, and she still struggled with what it meant. When she was around him, she tried to gauge the type of power he possessed and what unity meant. Yet each time she tried, she failed to identify it. All she knew was that Rob possessed something far more drastic and powerful than she'd ever experienced.

She bowed her head and looked around at the others seated. She had brought the massive, circular table from some deep part of the palace. This was once the throne room, though it also had not been used in that manner for quite some time. Her mother hated welcoming guests into the palace, so they didn't need a throne room. Her mother never welcomed *anybody*.

Serena's mother was rarely ever present in her life when she was younger. Her mother's presence was only felt in manifestations of power, which was her way of being there without being there.

"Thank you for asking my advice," Serena replied, nodding at Griffin while pushing aside the thoughts that crept into her mind. "I do appreciate you being here."

She strode over to Griffin, nodding at the faces she passed as she made her way to the other side of the table. There was Garthena, who was watching her with a slightly amused expression. An expression she often worn around Serena, lately. She still had an earthy quality, and was surprisingly powerful, despite not having a traditional type of fire essence. Still quite powerful, Garthena was incredibly skilled with her essence. Although Serena hadn't seen the extent of Garthena's essence, she'd seen enough to know that it was quite extensive, even for a dragon mind. She was one of the few people Serena thought she could help progress to dragon soul and was now trying to figure out what that would take. Her essence was quite different from Serena's, so Serena knew that she was going to need help with that.

Rob had a way of modifying essence, but she had never done it herself, and though she understood that life essence could transition and transmute other types of essence, she didn't know what that was going to involve for someone like her.

The other council members were high-level dragon minds and had been living in the realm for a long time.

Many of them had been enemies at times, but Serena had taken it upon herself to work with them, knowing that she needed to find a way to piece together a measure of trust, even though that task was particularly difficult.

Griffin tried to help and coordinated much of it, especially since he knew that Serena had been targeted by many of them. He tried to protect Serena, even though she was much more powerful than him.

Relthorn watched her with his hands clasped on top of the table. Though his features were unreadable, she knew that if she used her dragon ability, she could reach into his mind, take some of the thoughts that were there and peel them away. But she didn't want to dive into his mind, because she agreed with Rob that such a thing was a violation, even though there were times when she thought that having access to somebody's thoughts and what they were planning might be beneficial.

Then there was Jamial, an older leader of a once minor sect. Serena had offered copious amounts of essence to him and his people, which helped raise more of them, along with her standing, until they became far more formidable.

She walked past Alison, a young woman who raised to dragon mind faster than most of her sect. She was on the fringe of the sand sect until Serena started an alliance with her. She then took over as leader within her sect.

The rest seated at the table were members that Serena hardly knew. Griffin was the one who brought them into the council.

She took a seat.

The others looked at her, and each had a sense of

deference that radiated from them. Serena understood and accepted that it was because she was now the dragon queen in their mind, even though she didn't feel like the dragon queen.

"What is the purpose of this meeting?" Relthorn asked, leaning toward Serena.

She knew him the longest. At one point, Relthorn thought that they could be more than friends, but then he proved himself to be underhanded. Then again, he was trying to serve his sect, which was what her mother had trained her people to do.

She looked at each of them.

"The purpose of this meeting is to talk about my mother."

She felt the change in energy from the room. Uneasiness radiated from each of them, even though their faces remained unreadable.

"Why do I have to do this?" she asked through her dragon mind link with Griffin. He simply laughed at her.

"Because you are Serena," he replied.

"At least you're saying that I'm Serena, not the dragon queen."

She turned and settled her hands on the table, before leaning forward. She looked authoritative. She *was* authoritative. She had far more power than any of them. She was dragon blood, or whatever that meant. She controlled the essence that none of them could imagine. None of them knew what it took to be a dragon soul.

But she had to make them find it.

Rob had stressed its importance many times before. They had to find a way to help the others progress quickly so that everybody had the opportunity to understand the power that existed, and, more than that, so that they would be ready to fight. For so long, they believed the danger was coming from the Netheral, but it was an outside force, and they didn't understand and couldn't understand the power that this outside force held.

This time, she spoke aloud and with essence. It swirled around her and radiated toward the others. She needed them to feel the essence and hear her words.

"My mother has betrayed the realm," Serena said carefully. "And I've decided that it's time for the others to be aware of what my mother has done, and realize that the world has changed."

Murmurs erupted around the table as uncertainty radiated from their essence.

Serena waited, letting them have their moment. She focused on her own essence, letting it sweep out from her and touch each of them. Each time she did it, she felt the ongoing irritation they radiated.

But it was more than that.

She added different types of essence through the link, touching upon ice, life, earth, storm, water, and thorn. One after another. She didn't link or form them into a unity, but she wanted everyone to know her power.

The connection startled them.

"That was you?" Garthena muttered.

Serena nodded.

"Power continues to change the world. And I've continued to progress, learning about the power and my place with it. At this point, I am known as a dragon blood."

Relthorn perked up.

"Is that like your mother?"

"My mother could be," Serena replied, with a shrug, "but she has failed to see the truth in the world. She's been fighting the world's changes and has decided that she wants to have a different role in it. And so, she will be marginalized."

Laughter erupted around the table.

Serena turned her attention to those laughing and focused her essence on each of them until they fell silent.

Her mother used her essence to press down on others until they were overwhelmed. Something Serena had felt many times before, and she promised she'd never repeat. She wouldn't torment those working with her. She wasn't her mother.

If anything, she needed them to be comfortable with her role as leader.

Maybe I should bring Rob.

Rob was very powerful, and having him present might be enough, but…

At the same time, if she were to bring Rob, it would weaken her own standing. And she didn't want that. She wanted to keep strength and prove that she belonged. She wanted to have that power on her own without using Rob's manifested power. She was going to be Serena. Not the dragon queen.

"My mother has endangered us. She has endangered other realms. And she has sided with the one that we think attacked us. She is the reason that we've not progressed."

She looked at each of them in turn. Some of them had hunger in their eyes as they listened to her words. As a dragon mind, most of them thought it was impossible for them to reach the dragon's soul. There were quite a few dragon minds, and there had only ever been one dragon soul.

Growing up, Serena was told that there was no possibility of anyone else becoming a dragon soul unless the existing dragon soul were to pass on. For Serena, this would've meant her mother disappearing from the realm of leaving and dying.

Now they knew that this wasn't true.

"Progress," Serena continued, as her essence expanded outward, "That is what we're talking about. We must all find a way to progress."

"You would see us as dragon souls?" Jamial asked.

Serena turned to him.

An older man, Jamial had been a dragon mind for several decades. So, to him, reaching the dragon's soul after so long would seem impossible.

"I will try to create as many dragon souls as possible. And as you can see," she said, looking at Griffin, "we know the secret. We aren't going to withhold that knowledge. But we do need to make sure that those who progress to dragon soul are capable of helping and are willing to take what we offer and use it for the betterment of the realm."

The implication was clear, at least as far as Serena was concerned. She wanted them to know that it wasn't about just taking power and having power; it was about *serving*. That was the purpose of the power she and Rob had been chasing. They wanted power, and they wanted to progress, but they wanted it for a specific purpose so that all of them would be able to benefit from it.

It was different than what many others wanted for themselves.

Serena understood that, and she understood that there was far too much to the idea of progression that had been difficult, but she also understood that if they were to do this the right way, it was going to involve doing something that had not been done before.

"Why did you come here to talk with us?" Relthorn asked.

"Because you need to see."

"See what?"

Serena looked over to the door. It opened, and her mother was dragged inside.

Chapter Two

SERENA

Serena's mother had always been powerful.

Even now, as she stood, bounded in bands of a different essence, bands that Serena had placed and Rob had confirmed were secured, she still looked powerful.

She held her head high, her eyes fierce, and her hands curled into fists. Given that she was dragon blood and had entered the nexus with Rob and the others, it was possible for her to use some of the essence's bands. However, this would require her to attempt to use that type of essence and comprehend what had been given to her. Her mother had refused to learn about that essence, as she had wanted nothing more than to take the palace's power away from Serena.

A dozen manifested soldiers joined her, dragging her into the room.

Before, manifesting for the soldiers would be nearly impossible, as they were an extension of the palace, an extension of fire. However, now these manifested soldiers were drawn from the new power within the palace, the power of unity. Serena felt that power through the palace, the soldiers, and everything around her. It came from the link that she shared to the palace itself. That link allowed her to become a dragon soul, eventually leading to her ability to become dragon blood. What bonded her to the palace had continued to manifest and change for her, becoming something much greater.

The whispers around her pulled her out of her thoughts. She got up and stood at the head of the table. Griffin stood up beside her. She felt his uncertainty wafting in the air around her.

"Are you sure about this?" Griffin whispered.

She nodded, not taking her eyes off her mother.

"They need to know that I have the power to hold her."

"But you understand what this is going to look like?"

"It would look like I've taken my mother and held her. And that is exactly what I've done. They need to know and understand because they will need to trust that we can handle somebody like her."

She straightened her back and walked towards her mother.

Although she brought her mother before the council to show her strength, she also needed to break her mother. She could go into her mother's mind and try to reach the knowledge that she needed because she believed that there was something that the Eternal had offered her, or perhaps one of the other heralds, which prompted her to act the way that she did. Serena didn't know what that was, but she knew it was going to play a pivotal role in what they intended to do.

"What is this, Daughter?" her mother accused.

"Quiet," Serena commanded through her dragon mind connection.

Her mother recoiled, as Serena used her essence on her. She was not above using the same essence technique her mother used on her, as a means of torture.

"You're here for the show," Serena said aloud.

The room was silent as they listened to her mother's sharp breaths.

"I am not some sort of—"

Serena raised her hand, and her mother fell silent as she used her dragon mind connection on her.

"As you can see," she explained, turning to the council. "The dragon queen stands before you, chained in essence. While many of you may only be aware of the fire, I will tell you that there are bands of the other realm essences around her."

She proceeded to name them off, and as she did, she demonstrated the kind of power that she possessed, sweeping her head and arc, and creating a swirl of color.

The members gasped and whispered.

Most didn't know about the different types of essences; if they did, they didn't know that Serena could use them. This was part of the display.

"She thought that she would side with outsiders. She thought that we could not defend ourselves."

Serena glared at her mother as she continued.

"And she was wrong. We have deflected the attack."

"You have only slowed it," mother shouted, defiantly

before sneering at the others. "And all of you will suffer. Had you listened to me and allowed me to do what needed to be done, none of this would've happened. None of you would suffer the way you're going to suffer now."

"I think you should continue to be quiet," Serena warned. "You're making things worse for yourself."

She laughed coldly at her daughter's words.

"You think that I can't get out of here, Daughter? At what point will your man no longer be enough to hold me?"

Serena stiffened as her body trembled with anger.

"Enough," Griffin roared, appearing beside her. "You will not stand here and defile her like that. She has progressed, and *she* is the one who holds you. She is the one who came to understand the truth of the palace and the power that exists in the world. You will not deny it."

The room became silent.

Though Griffin's angry roar filled the room, the ferocity of his essence overwhelmed everyone. Though Serena and her mother were not affected by it, the power he radiated was too strong for the dragon's mind.

Her mother didn't know that Griffin was more than just a dragon soul. He had started to bond with the other powers of the realm, using the testing techniques they had discovered. Griffin was now bonded to most of the different essences, and though it would not make him dragon blood, it was a start. Serena hoped it would help him find a way to progress if that was what he wanted.

"You serve *me*," her mother hissed.

"I serve no one," Griffin said.

Serena's mother laughed. She tried flaring her essence, but the bands of power Serena had wrapped around her were too strong. Serena learned how to weave her essence from the palace's librarian, Tessatha. She taught her how to bind it to hold those of lesser or similar power. There were things Tessatha had known, certain things that she was still able to teach Serena, and Serena was always thankful for that.

"You always serve someone," she said, looking at Griffin with amusement. "You have always served. And if you're not serving my daughter or me, it means that you serve him. An outsider."

"Is that how you view him?" Griffin asked, his voice quiet. Dangerous.

Serena had never seen her uncle like this before. She knew he and her mother had never gotten along because he thought she was trying to use him, but this was something else. She could imagine Griffin lunging at her mother and using his newfound essence to destroy her. Given Serena's constraints on her mother, he could certainly harm her significantly.

"Is he an outsider?" Griffin asked.

"How could he not be?"

"A boy born in your valley," Griffin started, "and trained by those from your realm. Regardless of whether he has our essence, and I can tell you that he does, he is no outsider. The outsider is the one who refuses to recognize the power that exists in the world and refuses to do what is necessary when it means protecting others. All you ever cared about is creating dissent."

"All I've cared about is—"

"Enough," Serena said.

She felt a wave of her essence wash outward and realized that she hadn't been controlling it nearly as well as she needed to. That was dangerous, especially given how much essence she had. She withdrew it.

Maybe bringing her mother before the rest of the council was a mistake. It was too much. And yet, a part of her knew it had to be done.

"I'm not going to stand here and listen to the two of you bicker. We brought you here because you're going to listen to what we're planning. And you're going to reveal what you've been doing."

"I have done nothing," she proclaimed. "Other than what was needed for me to protect the people of my realm."

"By betraying them?"

Her mother scoffed.

"What you see is betrayal, dear daughter, I see as necessary. You will come to understand it, Serena."

Serena shook her head.

"In that, I'm afraid you're wrong. I have come to see the truth. I have come to feel the unity. I have come to know that even though we might be afraid, I also recognize that fear helps drive us to do greater things. Had I not been afraid of everything that I encountered, I wouldn't have pushed myself, and I wouldn't have pushed to become what I am."

She pointed to the others.

"And they wouldn't have pushed, either."

She held her hands out. "And now you will be a witness."

Her mother sneered at her. "Witness?"

"Witness to the next step," Serena said.

She looked at Griffin, who nodded. They had agreed that this would be part of the plan, though, with her mother's reaction, Serena didn't know whether it was going to be possible or necessary. At the same time, they felt as if they needed to do this. The next step was going to be difficult, and having her mother here was imperative, partly because Serena had decided that the essence, she was going to get to the others was going to come from the dragon queen herself.

She began to pull upon the essence.

It was fire, primarily, as all of them were connected to the fire. Her mother and Serena were both bonded to pure fire, as that was the primary essence that Serena had ever known and within pure fire was the power to use other types of fire.

She began to draw upon it, and it took her mother a moment to realize what Serena was doing. She was pulling fire off her mother.

"What are you doing, Serena?" she cried.

Serena ignored her. She pulled off that essence and began to pinch it free one by one. That was the key to what she was trying to do, and the necessary technique. Serena had seen Rob doing something similar, and had not really tried it herself, though she knew the technique was fairly straightforward. Her only problem was trying to seal that power into the others. It wasn't difficult to do it, but Serena thought that she might need to continue to push power and play some of it to hold it inside the others.

She started with Garthena.

She was the one within the council whom Serena felt closest to. She had the confidence that Serena needed. Without Garthena, they wouldn't have been able to stop the Netheral the first time.

She placed pure fire into her, forcing more and more of that essence, a gifted form of essence. But this time, it wasn't gifted from her, the way that Rob would often gift essence to the others of the north. Her mother gifted her this.

She could feel her mother's rage, but she ignored it.

She had no choice but to do so; she could feel that power coming off her, and the way it was radiating as it began to build upward. Serena recognized the power humming with vibrant intensity and began to intensify even more. Finally, she started to note that the energy going into her was considerable, and more and more, she began to push more and more until she could feel something pressing through her. The essence began to wash outward through Garthena.

Garthena gasped.

"What are you doing to her?" Relthorn asked, looking from one to the other.

Serena ignored him, pressing outward with a wave of her other essences, forcing them back in. At this point, the only thing that mattered was that she was trying to use the type of essence she had and to hold fire inside Garthena.

She wasn't sure all that was required, only that it had to be fully separated. It had to be a gift. That was the sprite that Rob had grown with, but it was also something else. It was some aspect of a higher power.

And that's what she was trying to do now. Find a way to make a higher power.

Essence allowed them to change. Essence had always been necessary for them to change, but transitioning to dragon soul meant a much more concentrated essence. And dragon blood, like Serena and her mother, had plenty of essence to spare, as they could concentrate it again, and did not have to worry about losing that control.

Especially not here, surrounded by all that power.

And that fire began to wash throughout Garthena. Serena pulled more essence from her mother, and as before, she pinched it off.

She didn't know if this was going to have any permanent effect on her mother. But even if it did, it wasn't a problem for Serena. She didn't care if her mother lost her power or could no longer hold onto the same energy that she had before. She simply did not care. She hated that she felt this way about her mother, but after everything that had happened with them, and everything that her mother had done, Serena simply did not care.

She placed this essence inside of Relthorn.

She figured that it would be easier to start with him after Garthena, partly because Relthorn was going to continue to question and partly because the others needed to see that she wasn't playing any favorites. They understood her frustration with Relthorn. She felt the fire flame inside of him and the way it was beginning to spread outward, radiating through his entirety. Each time she pushed, she began to feel more and more of that sweeping out from him, and then...

Then she felt it take hold. The power was considerable. She continued to press, washing outward, until the transformation began on its own.

Whatever was going to happen inside of Relthorn was going to take place without her influence. Serena could only do so much. The person receiving the gift had to find their own way to utilize that power. She might be able to force some of that power outward so they could continue to take on more and more of it, but there had to be an aspect of it that they were able to control on their own. And as she could feel, he was starting to do so.

She worked her way around the table, helping each of them, pinching the power from her mother, until it was done. Only then did she stop, and only then did she wait and listen.

There was soft, steady breathing from everybody. A gasping.

But more than that, there was the radiating of power.

She looked over to Griffin. "See that they are safe."

Then she strode out of the room, dragging her mother with her.

Her mother staggered.

Serena had pinched off quite a bit of power from her, which she realized in hindsight might've been more than what she should have done, but at the same time, she didn't care.

"You have wasted essence," her mother said between gasps. She spoke aloud, seemingly knowing Serena had blocked her and would not permit her to speak through the dragon mind connection.

She paused in the hallway, the door to the room now closed.

A figure appeared and caught Serena's attention. It was Raolin, and he was watching Serena, watching the dragon queen with an unreadable expression in his eyes.

"There is no waste," she said. "You understand that essence can continue to refill, especially for somebody of your power. So don't worry. You will continue to serve; only the way you will serve is going to be different than you had intended before."

"You intend to keep doing this?"

"I intend to see more of our people raised to dragon souls," Serena said. "Because that is imperative. We need to have as much strength as possible to defend our land. We need to unite our land. You may not have seen it, but Rob has. And I will do everything I can to help ensure that what we have learned, and what we do, ensures the safety of our land."

She then motioned for the soldiers. The manifested soldiers grabbed her mother and marched her back to the protected room Serena and Rob had created, which would hold her.

She turned to Raolin. "Was that too harsh?"

He approached slowly, radiating his dragon soul essence, the same as Griffin's. He hadn't gained additional essence as Griffin had, but not because she hadn't offered it. He chose not to.

"I think it was as harsh as it needs to be," he said, shrugging slightly. "I don't know if I would've done the same thing. Then again, this is your mother, who has hurt you."

"You've been hurt by her, too," Serena replied softly.

"Perhaps. Anyway, I came to you because I found something. It's something that I think you need to see. Well, not just you. The young woman that you've been working with, as well. And Rob. All of us need to go."

"Why?"

"Because this relic was not there before."

Chapter Three
SERENA

Serena found herself well outside her realm. At this point, though, Serena began to question if she even knew what her realm was. Rob would say, 'all of the realms were now interconnected'. She could feel some aspect of that; the interconnectedness made it so considerable power was everywhere. The unity.

From what she and Rob determined; the temples were used to prevent the essences from mingling in this way. It was as though they were built, so that other essences could not come together, and limit others from reaching this kind of power.

What purpose would there be in that?

If somebody did that, the real question was, why? Whoever did it, had done so with a purpose, and they must have wanted to impede someone else from gaining the power that they had. But that implied intent, and Serena certainly didn't understand it, but she was determined to figure out what it was.

She looked around, feeling the energy. This place sat beyond the boundary of Rob's lands, near enough to the thorn realm, and yet, she felt as though she'd been here before, and at the same time, she couldn't tell if she had. She felt a strange sort of power, yet that power was linked to something greater.

"Out here?" Tessatha asked.

She strode towards her, oddly dressed in a dappled green cloak and pants.

Serena smiled.

She had found a friend in Tessatha, and an unlikely ally. It surprised her, especially as she had never thought she'd meet anyone like this. Tessatha's experiences were from centuries ago, though she had been trapped in time, trapped with the power of the thorn and brambles, and had been corrupted over that time until Serena and Rob freed her and her mind. There were times when Tessatha still struggled, times when Tessatha still acted as if she were trapped, but most of the time, she was an incredible ally.

"This is where he said to come," Serena shrugged. "But I don't know where he is."

Raolin gave her directions on how to reach it but had not shared anything more about it, except that she needed to come out here. Serena thought it was a bit odd, but then again, her father was still odd. Ever since he had been restored to his essence and to something that was a strong semblance of who he had been, there had been part of him that had remained a bit unusual. Serena had taken that as the price she had to pay for everything he had been through. Surprisingly, though, he wasn't too upset about the fact that the Netheral still existed, and, more than that, that the Netheral had become something of an ally for them. He was forgiving.

At least, he forgave the Netheral. He did not forgive Serena's mother.

Serena still didn't know everything that happened between the two of them in their life before he disappeared, and she increasingly suspected that she never would. Maybe it was for the best. Maybe there were certain things she didn't need to know, as there were certain things she could not know. Her father was different, but had he always been different? Had he always protected her from her mother?

Serena didn't have the answers, which left her bothered.

"Something is different here."

"You can tell that?" Serena asked as she turned to her friend.

"I can tell that something feels a bit different," Tessatha answered. "But I'm not sure what it is, and I'm still trying to piece together what the different essence means."

Serena started to laugh, and Tessatha shot her a confused expression.

"I don't have any real experience, either," Serena assured her. "I'm borrowing from Rob, and I think he is borrowing from Arowend."

"Perhaps that's all it is. Arowend would have more experience with this, wouldn't he? That is, the old Arowend. I think he's still struggling with some of those memories. I wonder if there's any way, he could regain more of them than he had."

Serena had given that some thought. Arowend, at least in the form that they knew him in, had been trying to regain and gather some of the fragments of essence that had shattered during his destruction and death. And in that time, he had regained much of it, but not all. Serena didn't know if he could regain all his memories. According to Rob, there might always be gaps, the same way that there were always gaps with Eleanor.

"Anyway," Serena said. "He said there was some artifact here that wasn't here before."

"What kind of an artifact?"

Serena shrugged.

"He wasn't clear about that, and I think he was intentionally vague because he didn't want me to worry about it until we got here. I'm not entirely sure what it is, so…"

"Should we go and investigate?" Tessatha asked.

"Without anyone else here?" Serena asked.

Tessatha looked over, and she frowned, arching a brow. "Do we *need* anybody else here?"

Serena smiled to herself. *Did they?* She didn't think so, as she was certainly capable enough. Besides, she had Tessatha with her, and the two of them were capable of doing this on their own.

"No," Serena said, motioning for her to follow. "Come along."

They walked forward. They didn't fly, though they easily could. She sensed that Tessatha didn't care to fly, so Serena often chose to walk around her, as she didn't want to upset her new friend. Other than that, though, it allowed her to try to detect whether there was something else around her and whether something in that essence had drawn her father's attention. He was the one who had detected this, after all, and whatever it was, had been potent enough to draw him from inside of the fire realm.

Serena couldn't tell what it was, only that she could feel something was off. But it wasn't just off. The more she focused on what she felt, the more she was certain that what she detected was a kind of power that radiated a unique energy. It seemed to be the unity.

But not the kind of unity she could create. Her ability to merge the essences was how Rob had once been able to do it. This was something else. This was something pure—the way Rob could *now* do it.

"Have you ever seen the nexus?" Serena asked.

Tessatha glanced over, shaking her head.

"No. Arowend knew about the nexus and theorized where it might be found, but neither of us could uncover it. He said that it's deep beneath the ground, or in another plane of existence, possibly. Regardless, you'd have to manifest to reach it."

"That's what Rob said, as well," Serena admitted. "But what if this power is the nexus?"

"Why would the nexus suddenly reveal itself like this?" Tessatha asked.

"I don't know. Maybe because Rob created some sort of a natural unity?"

There was still so much that Serena didn't understand, and so much that she needed to try to make sense of, but even as she attempted to do so, she didn't know if the answers were going to be there. Instead, she went along with the flow, letting the energy guide her and allowing her to try to feel whether there was anything up here that she might be able to uncover.

She hurried along the path with tall, spindly trees lining either side. Further along, the trees disappeared, and oddly shaped rocks were piled on either side. She stopped as she felt the unity essence emanating from rocks. Closing her eyes, Serena focused on that energy.

Is this what father mentioned? she thought.

She thought back to his words. He spoke of a relic, which meant that the essence emanating from the rocks wasn't it.

"What do you think he meant by a relic?" Serena asked though she didn't really expect much of an answer.

"Maybe it's that."

Serena turned to where Tessatha was pointing at.

In the distance stood a tall, spiral tower made of a pale white stone. It seemed to loom out of the distance, looming out of nothing and nowhere, and…

And Serena had no idea where it came from. She'd never seen it before. It was a solitary finger of stone that protruded upward.

"What is that?" Serena asked in a whisper.

"That is what I suggested you come to find," a voice said, from behind her.

Serena spun and saw her father approaching. He wore a long overcoat, a leather satchel hanging on one shoulder, and a bit of a smile on his face. He looked comfortable. He was in his element.

And why shouldn't he?

Her father had always enjoyed wandering, exploring,

testing, and searching for relics. This was him and the gift he'd given her, as Serena had shared much of that with him.

"When did it first appear?"

"I'm not entirely sure," he said, glancing over at Tessatha and nodding politely. "As I didn't know about it previously. This was in no record I've ever found, and I think it simply appeared. This means that whatever Rob has done, changed things."

"But Rob wouldn't have simply erected a tower like this," Serena said.

Wouldn't he?

There were certain things that Rob was able to do and powers that he had, which Serena didn't fully understand.

Did he have the ability to raise stone like this suddenly?

After Rob progressed to this unity, something that Serena *still* didn't fully understand, there was a part of him that had certainly changed. His power was far more potent than it'd been before. He spoke of being able to erect barriers around the entire realm, including the ocean, with little more than a thought.

But how could anybody have that kind of potency?

And how could she ever understand him?

She tried to avoid those questions as they were difficult for her to think about, but at the same time, there were times when she got lost in that line of thinking, and she felt like she was trailing Rob for too long now. And at this point, she wasn't sure if there would be any way for her to reach that same unity. It seemed as if it were a singular thing that a singular person could reach.

Or perhaps this was her fear and anxiety speaking.

"I didn't have anything to do with this," Rob said.

It came through the conduit, yet she felt him, meaning he was close.

"Are you coming?"

When her father suggested that she see this relic, she'd reached out to Rob, but there hadn't been a response. That wasn't uncommon. Recently, she felt as though she was trying to chase him without really having any way of getting to him. Then again, Rob was busy. He was dealing with the Eternal and trying to question him, to come up with answers as to what he was after, and who this other entity was.

It was because of Rob and the memories that Tessatha and the Netheral had that they learned how to bind a person of similar power. He used the techniques on the Eternal that she used on her mother.

"I'm here," he said.

Moments later, Rob appeared.

He did so with such quickness, that she knew it was a manifestation. Still, there were times when Rob had manifested, and she had known that it was little more than a manifestation. Ever since he progressed to the dragon unity, or whatever it was that he called it, she was no longer certain. This could simply be his ability to transmute and change forms, given his control over essence, which didn't seem impossible to her. Not only that, but there was a physicality that was present now that wasn't usually present in a manifestation. She could do something similar, but not with the same potency as Rob.

He looked strong. He looked powerful. He looked... like Rob, who had changed so much over the last few years.

And maybe not even the last few years. It was easy to lose track of how much time had passed, as they had been going through so much and doing it so quickly that not much time really had passed for either of them. And still, when Serena looked back, she thought about how far she had progressed, but it was nothing compared to Rob's.

Raolin tipped his head, practically bowing to Rob.

Rob smiled tightly. "This wasn't here before," Rob said, nodding to the tower. "And yet, it does feel like it's connected to unity." He strode toward it, leaving the others watching.

"He's grown so powerful," Raolin whispered.

"He has," Serena admitted.

"Does it scare you?"

It was odd having this conversation with her father, but it was still odd that she felt as if she needed to have it was somebody. "Did it scare you being with my mother?"

"There were times when I was acutely aware of her power. Then again, I think she wanted me to be aware of it, as if she needed to have it as a warning, of sorts. She wanted to ensure I saw her as the potent one in the relationship."

Serena looked at Rob's back as she followed him, with Tessatha alongside her. She was quiet, though, through their connection, she was aware that Tessatha was listening.

"I don't think it's like that with Rob," Serena said.

And she was certain that it wasn't. Rob never wanted her to know that he was more powerful. Then again, for so long, he had not been. So, the change in status wasn't something that Rob really thought much about. At least, when it came to her, as she suspected, he was quite aware of it when it came to others.

"As long as you're comfortable with it, should it matter?"

"I just want…" She squeezed her eyes shut, and she frowned.

What did she want?

She wasn't even sure what it was, but then again, she was. When she thought about what she wanted with Rob, what she wanted with her life, she knew the answer. She wanted an equal partnership. Were they able to have an equal partnership when he was so much more powerful than her? There would be nothing equal at that point, would there?

Raolin touched her arm, squeezing softly.

"You want what everyone wants," he said, tipping his head toward Rob. "And don't fear it."

He strode forward and joined Rob for a moment.

Tessatha took Serena's arm.

"I understand what you're going through," she said softly. "I went through something similar was Arowend. He was always the skillful one. At least, he always had been before. I had a better mind, but a better mind is only good enough for certain things. He never made me feel that way, though. He always made me feel as if I were stronger than I was. I think that you must be comfortable with who you are, and the power differential is not insurmountable. The real difference is how you feel inside."

Serena looked over at her father. Was that the issue with her father?

But then...

She didn't think so. Her father never acted as if he cared that much about the difference in power. But then, why was there a struggle between him and her mother? Maybe the struggle had been the dragon queen. Maybe she was unhappy with the situation in some way. Or maybe... maybe Serena couldn't know.

They stopped at the tower and looked up. The type of essence radiating from it was unfamiliar to Serena. It was much like what she felt off Rob these days, something she could only detect if she were somehow connected to it, but she could not use the same power. Whatever it was that Rob possessed was so much different than what she possessed, as he had mingled his essence in a way that had changed him profoundly.

"The tower is radiating unity."

Rob nodded.

"It is."

"But it's not just radiating it," Tessatha said.

Serena followed Tessatha's gaze and saw the markings on the building.

"There are symbols here. They're old. Older than anything that I've seen and studied before."

That surprised Serena. "Older than anything that *you* have seen?"

She nodded, reaching out and running her fingers along the engravings.

"Much older. I recognize some of the basics, but the markings aren't anything that I would be able to do anything with. I think… Well, I think we can take some time and try to analyze it, but it might be beyond us without having any other records to access."

"We have the library," Serena said.

"Perhaps that will help," Tessatha said.

Rob frowned.

"What is it?" she asked.

"It's this," he said, and she felt a weariness from him. "It's the power of this. It's a simple fact of this. I thought we might have more time to understand what we were dealing with, and hopefully have more time to deal with the threat of the others, but maybe we don't."

"We knew there was going to be a danger," Serena said.

"I know," he said, with a soft sigh, "but that doesn't change the fact that I would have liked to have more time." He took a deep breath and let it out. "I need to speak with him."

Him. The Eternal.

"Be careful," Serena said.

"I have been careful," Rob said. "I think now it's time for me to be less careful."

With that, Rob vanished.

Chapter Four

ROB

Rob stood inside the vast empty cavern. He could feel the energy around him, emanating from everything and everywhere, a power flowing throughout the realm.

He was spending far too much time here, and now, he was starting to wonder if this was ever going to get him the answers that he wanted. He thought he needed to keep pushing, but he was also concerned about the lack of time that he was taking to make other preparations.

And now we have a strange relic that appears.

What did that mean?

It was unity. He noticed that immediately and saw some markings on it that triggered some forgotten memory inside of him. Rob must've seen them at some point before, but he didn't know why, what that might mean, or if it even mattered.

The fact that the relic suddenly appeared was worrisome, though.

And it was the kind of thing that was bound to suggest that there was ongoing power that was taking place and that, eventually, Rob was going to have to deal with it, if he was ever going to come to terms with everything else.

With a sigh, he turned and headed deeper into the cavern.

This was the only place that he'd been physically present lately. Well, that wasn't entirely true, as he did have to go out to eat, drink, and take care of the routine activities of life.

The cave was well protected, as he wanted to ensure that any place where he would bring a dangerous threat like the Eternal would be defendable. He was certain that no one could break in and cause harm to anyone within his realm, as he added the unity barriers as an extra layer of protection and the lashing of power, he borrowed from Tessatha.

Rob was thankful for those memories, as he wasn't sure he could do anything with the Eternal short of killing him otherwise. And Rob certainly didn't want to destroy him. At least, he didn't want to destroy him *yet*. There was still far too much that he needed to learn and understand to know what more they might need to do.

His mind worked on unity.

He could feel the tower now that he was aware of it and felt it protruding from the land as if it were trying to radiate some of that energy. Rob wasn't sure of its purpose, only that there was a pulsing of unity flowing through it.

Now, he needed answers.

As he told Serena, he had been careful with the Eternal, maybe too careful, as Rob began to question whether or not he would find the answers he needed by pushing too hard. And there was a part of him that hesitated to latch onto the Eternal's mind because he simply didn't know if he had the power to keep himself safe from the Eternal.

His next step was doing what he'd done with the Netheral initially, taking the risk. But he didn't like it, and he didn't like the possibility that something bad might come from it, but at the same time, he felt like he needed to take the gamble.

The central chamber was quiet. Earth had retreated for him, giving him space, and the other essences had all worked through here, all at Rob's command. That was a strangeness about his newfound power and connection to the unity. He was able to demand that the essences work for him and that they react in the way that he needed. It took little more than a thought. It didn't require any structure, not the way that it had when he had not progressed to this stage. Now everything seemed to happen simply, little more than a command so that Rob could direct everything into functioning how he needed it to.

He found the Eternal seated, but then again, he would be. There were a series of twisted essence bands around him. Rob had placed most of them, though Tessatha had helped, adding in layers of power around him, linking them in such a way that they would bind downward and hold so that the Eternal could not go anywhere. The Netheral had helped, using his fractured memories to try adding something to it. Together, the combined powers had held the Eternal in place. And it also began to diminish some of his essences, forcing a regression in power.

Although Rob hadn't reduced him to dragon blood, he was still manageable. The Eternal looked up, and a bit of amusement gleamed in his eyes as he often did. He seemed far more at ease with everything around him than he should be. That bothered Rob, partly because he felt as if he were not in control, though he wanted to be.

"You look like you have seen something that troubles you," he observed.

Rob made a quick circuit, testing the protections. Every time he came in here, he did the same thing, wanting to ensure that everything was as well defended as possible. He did not think that the Eternal had any way of overpowering that, but he also didn't want to take the risk. Not only that, but it was a simple matter for him to test those boundaries. It was a good habit, he suspected.

"I like to know more about this one you serve," Rob said.

The Eternal laughed. "I told you; you will learn in time. You think you've uncovered some great truth, but the only truth you've truly uncovered is that you're inconsequential. We all are."

That was part of all this that left Rob scratching his head and searching for answers, as he simply did not know whether there was hyperbole. The Eternal spoke about some great power, referenced that Rob couldn't handle it and that they were inconsequential. That was a frequent phrase he used. And if Rob and the Eternal were inconsequential, how much power did this other possess?

Far more than Rob could even fathom? However, Rob could fathom quite a bit of power.

"Why do you think it is more than I can handle?"

"I see what you've done here," he said, tipping his head toward the walls around him. "And I can feel the way that you're holding me. It's reasonable," he deduced. "But it won't last. You'll eventually slip, and I will escape."

"Or I'll kill you," Rob said.

He made the statement offhandedly and could feel the Eternal stiffen ever so slightly.

"You don't have that in you," the Eternal said.

Rob released a lashing essence, looping it around the Eternal's throat and squeezing.

The Eternal was strong. He was whatever this level was, dragon unity or something else, and because of that, anytime Rob tried to constrict the power around him, he could feel the energy resisting as if some part of the Eternal was potent enough to withstand what Rob was doing.

Not only that, but it seemed like there was some other aspect of it that he was using. Rob had always known reaching dragon skin level had made a person strong, but with the Eternal, it was as though it made him something else. Rob suspected the same would be said for him, which was reassuring to know that he could be difficult to kill.

Still, weakened as he was with the bands of essence that were looped around him, Rob continued to squeeze and constrict him. He felt the Eternal starting to weaken.

"I think you should revisit your belief of what I'm willing to do," Rob retorted.

He channeled everything he used when he fought the Netheral. This wasn't Rob's nature, but the Eternal didn't know that.

He released the band.

"Tell me about this other."

The eternal coughed, as he gasped for breath.

"You can't even fathom the power of it. No one can."

Rob smiled, as realization slowly set in.

"You don't even know, do you?"

The Eternal's body stiffened.

"I am the herald," he proclaimed. "I am the Eternal."

"And you don't know."

With that, Rob plunged into the Eternal's mind.

This was the gamble he was willing to take. He could feel the pressure as the Eternal tried to fight and expel him from his mind, but Rob pushed downward, using as much force as he could.

His mind was strained but not overwhelmed, as he tried to grasp the knowledge from the Eternal's conscience.

Rob opposed doing this with anyone else, as he didn't like the idea of violating someone's freedom and stripping through their memories. Connecting to a dragon's mind or higher was generally easy as they could protect their mind, and connecting to anybody lower would be dangerous because they could not. In this case, Rob knew there was going to be danger, and he used everything that he'd learned about the dragon mind's ability to probe.

The superficial thoughts were easy enough.

As he reached in, he saw the Eternal's anger and rage, but something else was within the depths of consciousness. Not only did the Eternal want to destroy Rob, but there was something else within him. Something unfamiliar.

Fear?

What did the Eternal have to fear?

Rob started to withdraw until something made him pause. There was something within the fear that was significant for the Eternal. And the fact that he felt that at the superficial thought, level suggested that he was in danger.

Not Rob. The Eternal.

He tried to plunge deeper, but stripping through the layers and diving into the Eternal's thoughts had been difficult for him. He simply didn't have the necessary skill at dragon mind level for him to be able to do so. Maybe some of the others would have more skills, and perhaps that was something that Rob would need to master so that he might be able to dive deeper and strip out some of the other artifacts so that he could understand just what it was that the Eternal was doing, and who he was protecting.

Himself.

He believed that the Eternal was trying to hold onto something because he feared for his own safety. But it wasn't Rob that he feared. This was from something else. Some*one* else.

"What is it?" Rob asked again, withdrawing from the Eternal's mind. "I can tell you fear it."

"As should you," the Eternal wheezed, his head drooping forward.

There was no bravado this time. It was a simple statement.

"I'm not the only herald. The others will come, and you will suffer."

"Will I?" Rob asked, leaning towards the Eternal. "You saw what I'm capable of doing."

The Eternal raised his head.

"And you've seen what I'm capable of doing. So, imagine five more. Imagine how that would feel. Imagine how your people will suffer."

The Eternal watched him, and his eyes had a dark hollowness.

"Imagine how quickly all your people will fall. And they *will* fall."

"Why?" Rob asked.

He had been trying to get to the bottom of the question since he started interrogating the Eternal. He felt as if there had to be some answer here, something more that would help him understand what was behind all of this. Why now, why his land, and why all of this?

"Because you have his attention," the Eternal answered. "I go where I'm sent."

It was a bit more than Rob had ever gotten, so Rob was thankful.

Getting the Eternal's attention was bad enough, but getting this other…

Rob didn't know what that meant, other than there was something terrible to it. And whatever it was, whatever it meant, was such that Rob felt as if he were caught somehow.

More heralds.

At least five more?

Rob had a hard enough time with the Eternal, and that was once he had gathered enough strength and had managed to surprise him. If war came, and they all had the same power, or even if they didn't, that was going to be difficult for Rob to handle. It was part of the reason that he had wanted more people to progress, as increasingly, Rob continued to believe that he needed them to progress so that they would be able to defend themselves against the kind of power that was coming for them.

But what would they be able to do?

Maybe nothing.

Secure the borders. Ensure the safety of this realm. And try to ensure that nothing worse happens. And that would be all.

That might be all he could do.

He didn't know how much time he had, but given the nature of the fear he felt from the Eternal, he knew that it wouldn't be that long. The Eternal wouldn't be as terrified as he was otherwise.

He looped another band of power around the Eternal, trapping him, and headed out of the cavern, before hurriedly emerging back above ground.

This was in the depths of an ancient temple, a place that had been buried long before. Rob had uncovered it, and converted it for his own purpose, thankful that very few people knew where to find it. Rob revealed it to only Serena, Tessatha, and Arowend. He didn't want anyone else coming into contact with the Eternal, because he didn't want them to deal with that kind of power, and he didn't want the Eternal to sway them somehow, if such a thing was even possible. Rob didn't know; because he didn't know, he knew he needed to be careful.

He found Arowend waiting for him. This part of the temple was broken. A bit of the old ruin had fallen and collapsed. The different powers of essence flowed in through this temple, and ever since Rob had formed the unity, essence had changed everywhere, including here. He could feel the flow of the unity and the flow of the essence radiating through here, leaving it filled with a significant sort of power.

Arowend looked over.

"Has he gotten any clearer?"

Rob sighed, shaking his head.

"Unfortunately, no. I tried to read his thoughts."

He could sense Arowend's fear at that, and Rob understood. They had already spoken about whether or not this was safe to do. They decided not to try because there was the possibility that the Eternal might have some way of overriding Rob's natural defenses, but seeing the tower, and feeling the unity coming from it prompted Rob to take a risk that he probably wouldn't have taken otherwise.

"You do that alone?"

"You can test my mind if you'd like," Rob said.

"Do you think that I need to?"

Rob shook his head. "No."

Arowend nodded. "I don't know if I can do much,

anyway. If you were corrupted, your power exceeds my own."

It was such a simple statement, but it was strange for Rob to hear from the Netheral. At least, the person who had been the Netheral. Rob had thought for a long time the Netheral was farther advanced than Rob, and while that was true to a certain extent, he wasn't nearly as advanced as Rob had thought at the time. He just had a better understanding of the different essence than Rob. And yet, he was an essence manifestation, or at least some part was an essence manifestation, and because of that, he had far more power than anybody else. It was that kind of power that Rob still didn't fully understand, as he wondered if becoming this form, and taking on this power, would permit him to do things that Rob could not.

"I'm not corrupted," Rob said. "He mentioned that there are other heralds, and I think he's afraid they are coming for him."

"Do you think it's possible?"

Rob sighed. "I think it's likely. We already know that we've gotten the Eternal's attention, and if what he's telling me is true and he's not the one that's controlling things, then it's not his attention we need to worry about. It's the person controlling him."

"And if you have?"

Rob took a seat and leaned forward. He focused on the essence all around him, feeling the faint tracings of the unity flowing here. It drastically differed from the essence he'd felt for so long in these lands. Rob appreciated how the essence flowed, how it was built, and all its power.

But somehow, it wasn't going to be enough.

And that was what it always came down to for him, unfortunately. As much as he wanted to believe that he would be able to handle anything if there was an entity that was greater than the Eternal, he wasn't going to be able to do it in this form.

"There is only one answer," Rob said. "We have to progress."

Chapter Five

SERENA

Serena stood outside of the unity tower, looking up.

It was the name she'd given it because she felt the presence of the unity essence. Rob left before she could get any answers. She felt the uncertainty permeating him and wondered if he was doing something dangerous.

She couldn't imagine, standing before the Eternal like Rob did. The very thought made her tremble.

The one time that she had stood before him, she felt the power that he possessed and saw the malice in his gaze. Somehow, Rob stood before him fearless. Not only fearless, but he also interrogated him, questioned him, and demanded answers.

That is who Rob had become.

And yet, Serena wondered if she was capable of being his equal.

She shook away those thoughts.

Serena needed to understand the tower. And thankfully, she wasn't trying to do it on her own. Raolin had taken out a notebook and hurriedly wrote down all the symbols. He was making good time as he worked his way around the entirety of the unity tower, marking what he saw, and copying it. Tessatha was doing something similar, but she was doing it with essence, tracing it in the air, and then flicking something so that it disappeared.

When Serena asked her about it, Tessatha merely shrugged.

"I appreciate your father taking notes," she began, looking over to Raolin, who was crouching down and now sketching an image of the tower. Her father's hand was steady, and the tower he drew was quite realistic. "But I don't have the same skill at writing or drawing, so I learned to do this."

"But what is this?" Serena asked.

"This is my way of tracking markings. It's a simple use of essence. And it doesn't take but a single form of essence. I could do this even before I had access to these others."

Tessatha continued to make the markings, and then they disappeared with the flick of her wrist.

"What are you doing with them?"

"I call it pocketing," Tessatha explained. "I realize that's not exactly what I'm doing, as I'm not placing them into a pocket, but I am placing them into some part of my essence so I can feel that power and use it later. I can remember the tracings that way. It's a trick, little more than that, and it allows me to keep track of the different types of the essence I found and the different kinds of power that are there." She shrugged. "Again, it's nothing more than a trick."

"What happens if you leave that essence linked to you?"

"It's not a matter of linking it to me. I think it's really a matter of forming an essence memory now that I talk about it aloud. And now that we've seen other things similar to that. By doing this, I can continue to form different essence aspects and track some of that."

"And then what?"

"Then I feel like I can keep an eye on this and use my own essence to help me understand."

Serena tried to do something similar.

Forming an essence memory seems strange, but then again, so much of what she'd done over the years seemed strange, so why should this be any different?

And what she saw Tessatha doing didn't seem all that bizarre, just something that Serena wasn't familiar with. She began to trace the same symbols, using fire, as it was the primary essence that she always defaulted to, and then focused on her own essence, flicking that to herself.

Surprisingly, when she did, she felt a surge of fire, and those markings remained sizzling inside of her for a moment. It was long enough that Serena could follow that marking, track the power, and feel some aspect of it in a way that left her feeling as if they lingered. Even when that power began to fade, she was still aware of it more so than before.

She smiled, and she looked over to Tessatha, who shrugged.

"An essence memory," Serena said.

"I guess that's what it is," she said.

"And I wonder if I can do this with other things," Serena said.

"I don't see any reason why you couldn't."

How much more could she remember if she were able to use essence memories in such a way? The idea had so much potential, and yet…

Yet Serena knew that she had to stop getting excited about the potential of something like this; she had to focus on the task ahead of her. She was here to understand the tower and try to make sense of anything within it. She continued to trace the markings, doing the same thing that Tessatha had been doing and focused on everything she saw, tacking it into her own essence to store it. She wasn't sure if she could hold onto it indefinitely, but she began to feel something more as she did.

After making a complete circuit of the tower, she looked over to her father, who had finished his drawing of the tower. She sat beside him, and he looked over, smiling at her.

"What do you think?" Serena asked him.

"I think this is something quite unique. We've not seen a relic suddenly appear before. Then again, we've not ever felt this kind of power in the world before, so it isn't terribly surprising that this would be unique like this. Do you think Rob is tied to it?"

"I don't know," Serena said. "These days, it's difficult to know how much of this is tied to Rob, and how much of this is tied to outside forces."

"Well, if it is the unity, and if that unity is tied to this nexus, then it suggests that there is an even more ancient power here than we ever knew. A power that has always been here."

Serena nodded. "That's my thinking, as well."

"Good," he said, and he nodded. "I was afraid that you weren't giving this proper thought."

"Really?" Serena asked, and she laughed. "You thought I wouldn't pay attention to what we were dealing with?"

Her father reached over and patted her on the shoulder.

"I just want to make sure you're actively thinking about things, and that you're prepared for the possibility that there is some other power here that we need to be concerned about. These temples were separate but allowed a connection, didn't they."

Serena nodded.

"And it's that connection I think is critical at this point because it seems as if the palace and perhaps his other locations, were all disconnected until Rob managed to link them once again. It was as if they were severed from the unity, or at least severed from the nexus. I don't understand what that means, but I think that's what we need to understand."

Serena nodded.

"I've been trying to work with the palace, trying to make sense of the power that has shifted inside of it, to see if there would be anything that I might be able to learn from it, but so far, I haven't found anything," she said. "I keep thinking that the answers are going to be there and that I'm going to find something, but…" She sighed. "The palace was working against us. At least, it was working against us until Rob used the nexus. Maybe the nexus is going to be the key."

"Or the nexus is just a manifestation of power," Raolin said. "And the real question is how and why the palace and other structures work the way they do."

Serena thought about returning to the palace, but she had recently spent quite a bit there. There wasn't any answer. If there was, she thought that she would be able to find it. It should be a simple matter for her to dive into the palace memories and search for anything she might be able to uncover so that she could track through them and realize the truth of it all, but so far, there was simply nothing. Serena didn't know if there was going to be any other way for her to find the answers that she was seeking, though.

There was somebody else, though, that she might be able to go to. She closed her eyes for a moment and reached through her connection, trying to connect to Maggie.

Finding the other dragon's blood was a simple matter. Serena knew Maggie quite well now, and connecting to her was a relatively easy process, though she could feel a distance between them even as she attempted to do so. She couldn't always tell what Maggie was doing, only that she was out there.

She waited.

"Come to me," Maggie said.

Serena sighed, and looked around for a moment, before manifesting to where Maggie was. It was in a grove of trees. They towered over her, the branches blocking out the sunlight. Serena could almost smell the forest, as she noticed the shifting shadows along the forest floor. Everything about this gave her a sense of power. It was life. It was Maggie.

And yet, she also didn't know if there was something else that Maggie was doing, perhaps hiding from her. There was no city or other part of the Borderlands, just the old woman's sense.

Gradually, an image of Maggie began to manifest, standing in the center of the trees. She was much like Serena had always remembered, with a wrinkled and weathered face, gray hair pulled up into a bun, and her cloak dappled and green, reminding Serena somewhat of Tessatha. That brought a smile to Serena's face. Maybe Maggie and Tessatha were more alike than she knew.

Maggie took a deep breath, something that Serena knew was unnecessary here.

"Something's happened," Serena said, sharing a series of images, filling her in on what Rob had uncovered. Maggie was quiet for a long moment, and when she finally spoke, she did so by looking around.

"I have also felt everything shifting around me," Maggie began. "It has been surprising. I do not know what it means, only that the changing of power around us is significant. I suspect it's what Rob has done, this unity, and…" She paused, turning back to Serena. "And I don't know what it means."

"You seem nervous," Serena said, realizing that was the emotion emanating from Maggie. That was an odd feeling, though. Maggie was never nervous. She was the one person that Serena could go to for answers and guidance. Even more so than her own mother, she realized.

"When everything begins to change, I think it's hard not to feel nervous. It is the only world and life that I know," Maggie went on. "And it's changing." She waved her hands towards the trees. "There is life essence there, but life essence is getting replaced. And once it's gone, what will it be?"

It was more than just what the trees would be, Serena knew. It was what Maggie would be. And it was a question that Serena had for herself.

What would she be once that unity essence pushed through?

Serena didn't know. She could feel that essence and the slow creeping of unity as it began to flow everywhere, even though she wasn't entirely sure what it meant. The only thing that she was truly aware of was that it was power. But was it an unknowable power? Not for Rob, as it was the kind of power he possessed, but for everybody else…

Looking over to Maggie, she saw that the other dragon blood was worried. She didn't say it, and Serena suspected that she wouldn't, as this was Maggie, after all, but there was something in her bearing, something in the way that she looked around, that left Serena thinking that was her real concern.

"Even within unity, there should be some sense of life," Serena said.

Maggie bowed her head.

"There is. And I can feel it. Even as it flows through here, and begins to chase the life essence that exists in my realm, I'm aware that there is something more. I just can feel something else to it as well. I begin to question. I don't know what Rob has started, and I don't understand."

"You fear it," Serena said.

"Do you not?"

"Ever since he stopped the Eternal and the attack, I thought that his chasing this unity was for the best. And…" She shrugged, as there was a different awareness of the world than before. Not only was their unity, but Serena was aware that the power she possessed and felt within Maggie also bridged in a manner that had not been done previously. It was that bridging, and that power, that Serena thought was necessary, and beneficial. By all of them had that same potential, everything would be different.

They would be different.

"I have had nothing but time to think," Maggie said. "Now we have this ancient relic that has suddenly appeared. We don't understand what it is, nor what it means."

"But it has to be old," Serena said.

"Almost certainly."

"But what does that mean?"

Maggie looked over to Serena. "The time that I can guide you has long since passed," she said. "There was a time when you first came to me that I thought I would be able to help guide you through your transitions, as I thought that was what your mother wanted. But I rapidly saw that there would be limits to what I could teach. And now I think you and Rob are the ones to provide me with the guidance." She smiled. "I'm afraid of what is changing, but I'm afraid in the way that someone who fears life has passed them by, is afraid. I don't want to stop it, and honestly, I'm not entirely sure that I can, but I'm not sure I'm supposed to be a part of it."

"But you're a dragon blood," Serena said.

"I am…" Maggie took a deep breath and looked up at the treetops. "But I am *tired*."

It was a different admission from Maggie, and Serena wished that Rob was there with her, wishing she had somebody to share this with, as Rob felt a closeness to Maggie that she understood. He felt as if he owed Maggie for everything that he had been through, everything that had become, much like Serena felt that she owed her to a certain extent.

"You don't want to face this other," Serena said.

"I suspect we will all be tasked with facing whatever it is to come," Maggie said. "But I do wonder if every change that has happened has brought us deeper and deeper into a path that we might have avoided."

"Now you sound like my mother," Serena said.

"I may sound like her, but I won't act like her. I recognize that there are certain things that I can intervene in and certain things that I should not. I will not try to prohibit what is happening. But…" She looked up again. "As I said, I'm tired. I wonder if perhaps my time is coming to a close regardless of what happened."

"Do you have anyone to replace you?"

"There are many candidates," Maggie said softly. "And yet… I feel like I want to see this through, if only to satisfy my curiosity. Whatever we see now is tied to something from the past. Something long before any of us, and perhaps it is so far before us that we can't even fathom what it might have been like."

Serena understood what she was getting at. It was the same thing that she had talked to Tessatha about. She had suggested that their knowledge of what they were dealing with was limited to her memories. Her memories might have been centuries ago and tied to a different set of knowledge, but in that time, there had been temples and power that they had not fully understood. So, anything they were dealing with now and still had to uncover was far older than anything they had seen.

"I'm looking," Serena said.

"I'm sure you have."

"I've been deploying manifestations. They were tied to the palace, but now that the unity has flowed through here, they're tied differently."

She could feel the librarian and his manifestations in ways that she'd not been able to feel before. Her connection to them was a little different, as well. It was part of the reason that she wondered if Rob might have a better connection to the librarian than she did, especially as he was the one tied to the unity, the palace, the temples, and the other places like that all throughout the realm that was now tied to unity, and not to individual types of the essence.

"And what have you found?"

"Nothing so far."

"And what has Rob uncovered?"

She focused on Rob, and now she was aware that he was quiet, almost pensive. As she focused through the conduit, she could feel his thoughts. That wasn't terribly uncommon, as Rob did not limit her from reaching his thoughts, and always made a point of keeping himself open to her as often as possible. In this case, though, she felt his worry, and she felt something else.

"I think he's concerned that we've gained the attention of something far more dangerous than we had before."

"If Rob fears it, then it must be true," she said.

"It probably is," Serena said. "And knowing Rob, I can only guess what he plans."

Maggie chortled.

"I don't know how that boy intends to progress this time. I didn't know what progression would look like the last time, but that is obviously what he's thinking of."

Serena snorted. "Obviously."

"And you?"

"I think that we all need to progress. Well, you can progress if you choose to, but we must fully grasp this unity essence."

"Yes. If we don't, our control will not be what it is."

"I haven't felt that."

"Haven't you?"

Serena hadn't paid much attention, but perhaps Maggie was right. She had known that there was some increased change, but even as she focused now, she started to feel for the different types of the essence and began to probe, wondering if there was any change she had not anticipated.

Maybe there was.

And if there was, it was certainly tied to unity.

Worse, if she didn't gain a greater understanding of

it, the power that she had, the power that she used to hold her mother in place—and the power that Rob was using to hold the Eternal in place—might not be enough.

"You feel it," Maggie said.

Serena nodded.

"Good. Since you feel it, you must work quickly. The essence is changing, and I fear we don't have much time."

Chapter Six

ROB

Rob sat and focused on the essence.

His awareness of it was quite a bit different than it'd been for a long time, and he began to feel for the power that was out there and around him. As he did, he began to feel as if there was something more he could uncover. As he strained and stretched his awareness, Rob recognized that there was a limit. Ever since progressing to reach this unity essence, a power that felt as if it were a part of him in ways that it had never been before, Rob had known there was a different limit than he had before. In this case, the limit came from how he embraced that essence and flowed through him, but also existed in how it was a part of the world around him. There was a point where essence no longer flowed and a point where he could not reach beyond.

He had been straining with it, trying to make sense of that power, and thinking that maybe there would be some point where he could feel for something beyond where he already was, but every time he attempted to do so, Rob realized that power was limited to him. It remained bound inside of him.

The Netheral was gone, having given him some space and the opportunity to focus more on the power he had been chasing. Rob appreciated that he did not push him, but also appreciated the fact that the entity that he had long known as the Netheral recognized that there were certain things that Rob could do that the Netheral could not.

But right now, it didn't feel that way.

Right now, it felt like Rob couldn't do the things that he wanted to do. He had been straining to make sense of it all, hoping that he could find an understanding and find a way to master all the power that was within himself, but so far, he continued to run into those limits.

What else was he supposed to do?

He had the unity tower, which he needed to understand. Why it suddenly appeared was a mystery to him, though Rob suspected that it was still tied to his type of essence. Somehow, having unified the land and bridged the powers here, everything had changed for Rob and some aspects of the land. More and more, Rob began to feel as if that change was the reason that the heralds and whoever they served had been drawn to him.

Somehow, all of this was tied to power.

But how, and what kind of power?

Those were the questions that Rob didn't have an answer to, though the questions that he thought he needed to try to piece together so that he could understand what he might be able to do.

He told Arowend that he needed to progress, but at this point, Rob didn't know what that would look like. He had this strange, unified essence and was aware of the power in ways he had not been before. To the point where he merely had to think about what he wanted to do with essence, and it happened. That was so drastically different from what he had done before, and it felt like he possessed something far greater than he ever had before.

But there was still something more.

And there was some other power that he needed to master, some of the power that existed out there, that he was going to have to counter, but he was going to have to do it with help.

He'd been thinking about how he was going to be able to get the others around him to progress, but at this point, Rob wasn't sure what was going to take. Maybe they would have to go into the nexus like he did, but she was hesitant when he suggested it to Serena. Perhaps afraid, though Rob wasn't even sure if that was the case. She had implied that it was more about a lack of understanding as to what she might find and about a danger that might exist there, hidden within the nexus. And for that matter, Rob realized that she probably was right. He had been to the nexus twice now, and each time he had come out of it changed, in a way that he couldn't even fathom. If another of the dragon blood that had gone with him were to enter it, maybe they could also find unity.

The dragon queen probably would, Rob thought.

He pushed that thought aside. He didn't need the dragon queen going into the unity and creating another problem for him in his realm. He needed to keep her restricted, so she didn't continue challenging them. And challenge them, she would. But the others, including Gregor, the storm cloud, and Maggie, could all have an opportunity to enter the nexus and see if there was any sort of power they could draw upon. They had not yet, which was unfortunate.

While he was sitting there, thinking about the different kinds of power that existed, and if there was any way he could coax the others that were working with him, Rob began to feel a strange presence along one of the borders.

Rob monitored it constantly, in case one of the heralds tried to attack him and his realm. So far, there'd been nothing, but Rob knew an attack was still imminent.

He also knew he couldn't stay. It was too dangerous for his people if he kept lingering. He needed to push back.

He stepped outside of the temple ruins, listening to the wind howling around him. The night was dark, and the air was cool. All around him was the sense of unity, the essence that he had mingled together, and Rob could feel how it was spreading out and around him, straining beyond the boundaries of where it had been before. He recognized that power and what he might be able to do with it, and recognized…

He recognized that, more and more, some aspects of it had been changing. Increasingly, he realized that he was going to have to talk to the others to see if their connection with their essence was changing as well. The fact that he had modified the essence by this connection to the nexus, unifying it into this unity essence created from the natural essence, might not be accessible to others quite as well as they once had been. That could be dangerous, and it was something that Rob hadn't even considered before.

The presence continued to push upon him.

Rob took to the sky.

It was a simple matter now. There was a time when he would've flown on lightning, and then used ice or one of the other essences so that he could travel, but now he simply burst upward, feeling the power of essence carrying him with little more than a thought. And then he traveled to the border, crossing over the water, aware of the distant sense of water essence down below, the hammering of waves and the spray that existed there.

He moved as quickly as he could, which was much faster than he once would've been able to do. When he reached the border, he was prepared for the possibility of a fight but did not see any gathering of dangers.

He moved along the border, continuing to test it. He *had* felt something. He had to find it. The night was dark. Even the moon was hidden behind a blanket of clouds, giving everything an ominous feel. Rob pulled upon the unity essence, drawing it into himself and then simply being. There were times when existing with essence was better than anything else, and in Rob's case, he could hold onto that essence, he could feel it flowing through him, and he could simply exist with it, letting it fill him, flow through him, and give him an awareness that he didn't have before.

Distantly, there was the sense of Oro and the other

water essence, and even beyond that, Rob could feel his realm and the land. He could feel everything that was coming from it as he strained to try to make sense of it. Every bit of his connection, every bit of his being, bound him to what he was feeling, and the way that power continued to expand behind him. There was great energy there.

He did not feel anything amiss in his realm.

The only thing that felt different was the presence of that unity tower, a beacon that seemed to burn within his mind, blindingly bright, as he focused on the essence. He could feel that even without focusing on it. It existed out and around and continued to call to him as if the tower itself were trying to draw some part of himself into it.

Was it trying to drain essence from him?

He stopped, floating in place, and focusing on the power that existed, as he started to wonder if perhaps the tower might be more than just a tower, and perhaps a weapon that the heralds' master had erected. If that were the case, how would they have an opportunity to place it in his realm?

And it did seem as if it were tied to whatever it was that Rob had done with the essence, binding, and combining it together so that it was more than it had been before.

No. It was not tied to the heralds. This was tied to what Rob had done.

He had to intentionally calm his mind, trying to shut down the awareness of that beacon that was there, as the more he stared and focused on it, the harder it was for Rob to feel for anything else. There was simply too much power within it pushing upon him, trying to gain his attention. Rob had to ignore it, somehow. He struggled with that more than he had realized.

When this was over, Rob knew he needed to go back to the tower and try to make sense of why he was feeling so much power from it, and why it seemed as if it were so connected to him in a way that left him practically trembling.

Once he shoved that awareness aside, he began to feel a strange pressure again on the border. It wasn't where he thought it was, and he hurriedly traveled, pushing himself off with a blast of essence energy that carried him to where he detected it. As before, the boundary was empty. There was no sign of attack.

Rob stayed in place, focusing, and when the next pressure began to build, he immediately reacted, bursting toward it. This time, Rob was almost on time. He was aware of the essence and power that was there, but he wasn't sure what was responsible, only that there was a considerable power.

He tracked that power, rather than waiting. And then he began to feel where it was flowing. It flowed along the border, but not consistently, bouncing from place to place and creating something of a pattern around. All of it worked along the water, which surrounded Rob's entire realm, but it continued to push inward, trying to overwhelm Rob's connection.

When he emerged from this attack, he was ready this time.

A strange-looking creature appeared.

Strange was the only way Rob could describe it. It

looked as if it were a mixture of a human and a bird, with a massive beak and wings that spread from its back but also had arms and legs that looked manlike. It was completely nude and covered with a faint gray fur. Something was horrifying about it, but more than that, it was the power of the essence that radiated. For a moment, Rob thought that this might be another of the heralds, but when he probed it with his own unity essence, he found that while it was powerful, it wasn't quite as powerful as the Eternal.

The creature battered its wings momentarily, watching Rob as if trying to decide what to do. Rob was tempted to attack, but then again, it didn't seem as if this creature would get through his boundary, so there was no real point in him doing so. He didn't need to destroy, did he?

Could he drain its essence?

Such a thing was possible, as Rob had done it many times, but in this case, he wasn't sure if draining the essence of this creature was going to be the right strategy for it, or him. He also didn't know if it would anger the creature.

But another thought troubled him just as much. He had made mistakes about others in the past and had believed that others were filled with dangerous power, and he attacked them, only to find out later that they were not his enemy. Not only was the Netheral not his real enemy, though at the time he had been, but Alyssa had proven not to be one. What if this creature was not an enemy for him, either?

The creature watched him, and then there was a horrible shriek.

Rob had to shield his ears, using essence to protect himself and his mind. Some part of the essence radiating off the creature tried to attack Rob's mind and shred through his essence, but Rob was strong enough to protect himself, at least within his realm. He wasn't sure what would've happened if he were anywhere else. And that worried Rob.

"What are you?" Rob asked.

The creature continued to flap its wings, watching. It hovered in place, looking like a strange insect. It watched Rob with eyes that seemed to burn with power.

Was this a herald?

He couldn't tell, and without having an opportunity to question the Eternal, Rob wasn't sure that he would know.

He was tempted to try to reach him through his connection and see if this was one of the heralds, but he decided against it, not wanting to risk having the Eternal have a link to him. Rob had been very cautious, knowing that if he permitted such a connection, there was a possibility that the Eternal might use that to escape. And given where he was held, and the access he now had to Rob's land, escaping meant others would be in danger.

The creature shrieked again.

This time, Rob was ready and maintained his focus, shielding his mind.

There was no response, otherwise.

"Are you one of the heralds?" Rob asked.

This elicited more reaction from the creature than

before. Its wings began to flutter faster and faster, and it waved its arms in a way that struck Rob as very unusual, to the point where Rob could feel some of the essence it was trying to generate. He had no idea what it was doing, only that he could feel it, and he could feel the way that the creature tried to draw power from its surroundings.

Not just that, but it seemed to Rob that the creature was trying to use the energy to break through Rob's boundary.

"You can't break through it; I've fortified it?"

"And you will fail," the creature said.

Rob looked at the creature with wide eyes.

Its voice was normal. A little deep, slightly hoarse, but quite human. How could it speak through its beak?

"Because of whom you serve?" Rob asked, "Your master isn't going to be able to stop this."

He wasn't as overly confident as he sounded, but Rob suspected that taunting him, even a little bit, was the only way to get answers.

"Do you think you're strong enough?" the creature leered.

"I'm strong enough to stop you," he replied, nodding at the boundary, "You can't break through this boundary. Otherwise, you would've already done so. I could feel you testing it."

The creature flapped its wings again, and its beak bounced forward as if it were pinching something out of the air. He could feel the pressure its beak had on the boundary. Rob had to be careful now. He didn't know anything about this creature or its capability, only that it was tied to the same entity the heralds served.

And if that were the case, Rob had to be especially cautious.

"They will come. And you will fall."

"They?" Rob asked.

There was only one thing he could think that this meant, but if it was the heralds, why was this creature here? Was it simply to test his protective barriers?

Or was this similar to what happened when the Eternal attacked? At that point, there had been others that had been sent ahead. They had attacked, and it was only because of Rob and his ability to fight them off, that protected the realm at that time. If there was something similar now, and if they were continuing to try to press, could he protect the realm again?

More than that, he had to wonder if it was going to involve the heralds bringing multiple agents of power.

"They will come, and they will claim this place."

The creature shrieked and clawed the boundary, slamming its beak against the barrier. Rob covered his eyes, as a small explosion erupted. He pressed the unity essence outward, fighting the area that the creature was attacking. The boundary was beginning to bulge. Rob drew everything from within and aimed his power at the creature.

The creature spun around and flew away. Leaving Rob alone at the boundary.

This wasn't about him, at all. It was about his realm. It was about the power that he had generated. And, he suspected, it was about unity.

The real question was, why? What did this creature want, and what could Rob do to stop it?

Chapter Seven

SERENA

Serena stood along the border of the fire realm, feeling the connection between it and the Borderlands. She hadn't spent much time here. It was a place where she had come to fully appreciate the extent that others would go to acquire pure essence. She understood pure essence but had not truly known what others would do to obtain it.

Do I even know now?

After all this time, Serena still wasn't sure that she did. The type of essence she had, and her access to essence, was so different from others. And this place had served as something of a beacon, becoming the first place where she had noticed the differences in essence availability.

This was where she and Rob had first begun to realize that there was more power in the world than she had ever known, and she had not returned since then. She was so focused on everything else that she had been doing and had not paid much mind to the strangeness that had been here at that time, the way that it was all connected to the pure essence that they had gathered, and which her mother had seemingly permitted the Sultan—Maggie—to have.

Now that she was here, she remembered what she had done then, and she was left wondering why her mother would have permitted that then. It didn't make sense with what she knew about her mother. Her mother was the kind who would gather essence and try to hoard it so that she would be the only one who could use it and have an opportunity to hold over others. Allowing the Borderlanders to have essence gave them the strength they wouldn't have otherwise. Did her mother have an ulterior motive?

She stood in front of the tower providing the entrance and where she had very nearly perished. This was where she had been betrayed. At the time, she was hurt by it, to the point where she didn't want to return to her homelands. She had not done anything with that hurt and had certainly not refused the others access to the essence she brought to the kingdom, but she was aware of those feelings now that she was here.

Rob would tell me to let go.

Then again, Rob had never ruled the way that she did. He had never seen an attempt at betrayal. He had never lived with someone and seen them use their knowledge and power against him. Rob didn't know what Serena went through…

But Rob still had a forgiving nature, and it was one that Serena had to emulate. She couldn't be the petty dragon queen. She wasn't even a dragon queen at all. She wasn't sure what she was, as she was still trying to decide if she wanted to be the dragon queen, but at this point, she didn't think that she was ready.

She stepped forward and began to press out with essence, drawing it through her. She had been testing different places, trying to make sense of what existed around her, and around her realm, to see if there was anything that had changed dramatically. Every place that she had gone so far had been much the same. There was something different that was no longer the way it once had been. Serena wasn't sure if that was a problem, as she could still reach for fire, along with each of the other essences, but when she did so, some parts of them felt different.

It felt as if she were tapping into something greater, but at the same time, she felt *smaller* somehow.

Perhaps that was part of the problem. And perhaps if Rob were around, she might be more aware of what she was detecting. Rob wanted her to be aware of the unity, so he would probably even encourage her to keep using the essence to get a greater understanding of it, and then be able to use it in ways that would help her people, and the realm. But what would happen to those who had not reached her level of progression?

That was the part Serena didn't have the answer to, and it was the question she thought she needed to understand. If her people were weakened because of the unity, and if none of them could reach for fire, then…

Then perhaps the unity might have been a mistake.

Would it make sense to weaken my realm?

As soon as she had that thought, she realized the folly of it. It was the same sort of thought that her mother would've said, and Serena hated having thought something that her mother would've. She didn't want to be worried about that kind of danger, as she didn't think that weakening her realm was the same consideration as it had been before. They could strengthen her realm, and her people, if they were able to reach for something more, a greater power. They could become a part of something different if they could find some way of being more like the ancients that had preceded them.

Her essence flowed into the ancient ruins.

As soon as it did, Serena began adding other essences. The last time she came here, she only had fire essence, but now that she had access to each of the other types of essence, she could feel how the ruins were bonded to those, almost as if each of those essences were meant to be used here. She continued to let some of that power flow out of her, and into the stone, which caused a series of markings to illuminate along it.

She froze.

She was certain those markings had been there before, but now that she stood there, feeling the power that was within them, she couldn't help but feel as if there had to be something more that she had not yet identified.

Maybe if she could blend the essences together?

She couldn't use the unity the way Rob could, but she could certainly twist the essence together and try to use them to help her build up enough power to create something more. And if she were to do that, maybe she could bind them together in a way that would allow her to find a way to bridge the essence together so differently than she had and find some other way here.

She started twisting the essence, beginning to bind them, using the techniques Arowend had taught and bringing the essence into unity. Once she brought each of them together, she felt the surge of power. Then she pressed that into the stone.

The writing changed.

The letters were different when she used each of the individual essences, compared to now, where there was a singular type of writing. She used an essence memory, trying to hold onto that and retain those memories, but it was difficult for her to do. She tried to use what Tessatha had taught her, but even as she did, she could feel that some aspect of it wasn't quite right, and though she was attempting to hold onto the memories, it slipped away from her. It was almost as if there was something to this essence, something to the way that she brought it together, that prevented her from using it as she wanted.

She paused again, binding the essences once more together, and trying to twist them in such a way that would bridge them. Each time she attempted to do so, she could feel the power working, then slowly slid them into the stone. She started from the base and worked her way up. There were a series of doors around the base, and she could use that, she thought, to try to make sense of what was there. As she did, she felt some part of that energy beginning to flow into the stone and upward.

She felt a strange sensation.

It felt as though the essence was fighting through the

stone, or a part of it was trying to battle with her. She focused on that, and the markings appeared. While keeping her focus, she hurriedly pulled out her notepad and drew them. This was much easier than trying to make essence memories. Maybe what she had to do was a combination of the two, using essence in her notepad. Wasn't that what she had seen as some of the ancient books, after all?

She wrote them down, working as quickly as she could through the markings, as she tried to ensure that she had them documented as quickly and accurately as possible, then pushed further up the wall, and more markings appeared. By the time she reached the peak of the ruins, she had made many different markings in her notebook, and yet, none of them made much sense to her.

Perhaps they didn't have to.

At this point, it was merely a matter of documenting. Serena was trying to understand what was out there and what the ancients might've understood. That's what they were trying to find, after all. She had been struggling with her own purpose, but in all that time, she hadn't been able to figure out what she was supposed to do, nor was she able to figure out what the ancients had done. The only thing that she had figured out was that there had been a time when power had been as it was now.

Then something changed, and that change bothered her, as it had either happened intentionally—and if that were the case, then Serena had to figure out why the ancients had decided they needed to separate their power—or it had been done to them.

She finished her notes, worked along the stone, and finally released her essence. When she did, she realized something. The stone of the tower itself had changed. It was almost as if she had begun drawing some unity into it. She could feel that essence and the way the stone was taking on a pale white, starting to glow, and it reminded her of the unity tower they had found.

But Serena didn't think that she had done that.

She had simply activated markings along the temple and had changed it. And if that were the case, then perhaps she was the one responsible for what had happened here, and perhaps she would be responsible for altering it more.

What if she were to do the same thing with the temples scattered through the fire realm?

She sighed, stepping back. There was the temptation to go to the chamber below, but Serena didn't think anything was in that chamber. Where would she go, after all? There was power there, or there had been, but now that the pure essence had been stripped away, she doubted that there would be anything more for her to go to.

But pure…

The unity.

For a long time, her people had often wondered about the difference between pure essence, and purifier. And there was a difference. She had never really understood it at the time, and when she was here before, she thought that there was something to it that she might be able to understand and that her mother might have known.

But maybe she hadn't.

She stepped forward, activated the door, and walked into the darkness. She hurried through the familiar halls, remembering when she'd been abducted, taken down here, and nearly destroyed. All because they had wanted to trade her for essence. By the time she reached the lowest chamber, she had found it empty.

The walls glowed, though. There was a bit of energy here that reminded her of what she had felt when she was here before, and some part of that lingered, giving her a sense of the power that had existed, and a sense of something more. Serena could feel…

Pure.

Wasn't that what she was trying to feel, after all? She could feel some part of that essence, she could feel the way that it was flowing, and she could feel it attempting to press upon her.

Pure.

Maybe that was what unity was.

If that were the case, was it dangerous for them to stop it? That had been fear, but Serena increasingly began to wonder if the purity of essence wasn't the problem. If her people could draw upon the unity, or pure essence, if that was what it was, then perhaps they would have an opportunity to use any type of essence they wanted. And that was a considerable benefit. Serena had never even considered that it was a possibility. Yet, standing out here, and feeling the energy around her, she was left with the realization that perhaps she should have.

She smiled to herself. All of this was potent and

powerful, leaving her feeling as if perhaps Rob had been right.

Each time she doubted him, she began to find other things that brought her back to his line of thinking. This temple. Maybe there would be others. And if there were, could they create other places of pure essence?

Could they use that so that others in her realm would have access to that power? And would they be able to find a way to help others use that essence to gain the kind of power they would need to become something more?

That was what this was all about, after all.

Everybody needed to try to find a way to be more. Serena had to, as well.

She hurried out of the temple, and paused for a moment, feeling the energy all around her.

It hadn't changed that much, but she could tell that there was some part of the unity, some part of that pure essence, that still lingered. And the more she felt that the more certain Serena was that what she felt was important. Somehow.

She hurried forward, traveling into her land, and to another one of the temples. It was not one of the peripheral temples connected to the palace, but this was an ancient ruin she had visited a long time ago with her father. It was small, sections of the walls had crumbled, but an opening remained within it, reminding her of the temple's ruins where her mother had hidden.

As she did, she immediately began to pour the different types of essence into the stone the same way that she had at the edge of the Borderlands. She felt the change and realized that much like the last one, something more happened when she created the unity essence and pushed it. It was almost as if it locked the essence together and allowed her to create something different.

A pale white began to work its way up along the stone. Then a strange connection formed. When it did, Serena felt it differently than in the Borderlands. Maybe it was because the Borderlands were at the edge of her land and because she did not have the same natural connection as she did here. As she formed that connection, she began to feel that power bubbling outward and radiating through.

Then the temple seemed to tremble. It bubbled with the energy of unity.

But another connection formed.

Serena was aware of it because of her connection to the palace. This unity shifted, and some part of it seemed to link to the palace the way that it had not been before. It allowed the palace to focus on unity.

The unity was pushing outward, pulsating from this temple, spreading throughout the land faster and faster, changing the connection, changing the link to fire, and drawing it instead into unity. Serena could still feel the fire, but she wondered if others who were only connected to fire would be able to feel the same thing, or if what she had done would have severed some aspect of their connection, changing it so that they were no longer able to reach it.

Perhaps this was a mistake.

And until she knew, she was going to have to keep testing.

Chapter Eight

SERENA

Serena stood near the palace, embracing the pulsating unity from the temple she had changed along the border. There was enough power within that temple, drawing from the unity, but probably drawn from the nexus. Serena seemed to have some sense of direction from that power as it flowed outward and began to work toward the palace itself. Some parts of the palace were beginning to shift in a way that they had not been before.

When Rob had gone into the nexus and done whatever he'd done there, the palace had changed. And now she was able to reach it much better than she had before, but ever since that, she had not attempted to connect it or link it in any way to the unity, not how she was feeling now.

But now she was noticing that the power was beginning to slowly flow as if some aspect of that unity was flowing toward her and the palace. Serena wondered if the same thing needed to happen here or if it would be too dangerous for her to do so. She had seen the markings along the temple walls, but she didn't know if there would be something similar here. If there was, then she might need to do something to help draw upon that power, but she was also concerned that if she did, some aspect of it would change, and she would modify the palace in a way that she would not be able to reach for the power that she knew that was within it.

She headed inside. The manifestations of the soldiers stood motionless. She hurried up to the room where she kept her mother prisoner. She was curious as to her reaction.

When she opened the door, she found her mother pacing. Her mother was rarely agitated. But today, her hair, which was always tied in a pristine bun, was now loose and frazzled, and her eyes were wild, crackling with fire, but…

More importantly, she seemed to be holding onto the power within her, but not able to reach for anything more.

Her mother turned to her the moment she walked into the room. Serena had not come alone, having brought several of the manifested soldiers with her, knowing that it was dangerous for her to risk coming to her mother without having any sort of help. When her mother saw them, she snorted before continuing to pace once again.

"I suppose you know what you did?"

"I know what I did," Serena said.

Only…

Serena didn't *really* know what she had done. She could feel it even now, though. It was almost as if the palace itself was trying to speak to her, warning her about some part of it that had changed. Every passing moment it continued to add more and more change, to the point where Serena felt some parts of the palace pulsating with unity, and no longer pulsating with the same presence of fire as it once had.

"You will change *everything*," her mother said, glancing over at her. "He will destroy everything that we have become."

"Or I will make everything better than what it had been before," Serena said.

Her mother snorted.

"You're so foolish. So arrogant. You think you know everything but know so little about this land and what came before you."

Serena paused, and she glanced over at the soldiers. With a flick of her head, they all departed, leaving her alone in the room with her mother. It was a gamble, but at the same time, it was probably the right kind of gamble, as Serena knew that her mother was not going to speak as openly with the others there. Not only that, but she also thought that she needed her mother to feel confident in a way that she only could when she thought she had the upper hand on Serena. With the soldiers present, she would not feel that way.

"If you knew so much about this land, then you would've understood what was here before. You do not."

"I understood the power that was here. I simply did not…"

She paused, and when she did, Serena watched her for a moment, trying to make sense of what her mother was thinking, but there was no obvious sense from her. Rather than trying to push through a dragon-mind connection, she simply waited, allowing her mother to try to share more. When she didn't, she looked around and started to pace with her mother.

"You understood the power that was here, but you didn't connect to it?" Serena asked. "Why?"

"I didn't know how," her mother finally said.

Serena smiled to herself. That had been what she had long suspected, though there was another aspect to it, and it was something Serena wasn't sure her mother wanted to hear. It might not be just that her mother hadn't known how to connect to it; it might've been that the palace had not permitted her mother to connect to its power.

There was some aspect of the palace having a measure of consciousness. However strange that seemed, it had been difficult for Serena to comprehend, and even more difficult for her to work with as she continued progressing from dragon soul to dragon blood. The palace itself had given her some of that power. But it also tried to take that power away when it felt threatened.

"Now that you know what it could be, how do you feel?"

Her mother paused and crossed her hands together, looking over at Serena. "If you think I'm going to give you some great respect or credit for what you've done, you are mistaken, Daughter. I think you're doing the wrong thing. You know what's coming."

"That's just the problem," Serena said. "We don't know what's coming. We know something is out there but don't know why it's coming for us."

Her mother snorted.

"You understand so little. There is power beyond anything that you can fathom. I have felt it. I have dreamt of it."

This was something that Serena had not yet heard, and the idea that her mother dreamt of power left her with a different series of questions than she had before. Maybe what she needed to do was to ask her mother about that.

Why did her mother betray them and join forces with the Eternal?

Perhaps power?

No. She would've stayed and worked with Rob if it was about power. It meant that it was about something else. She wasn't sure what that was, only that it suggested that her mother needed something more.

And if it wasn't about power, was it about fear?

"Are you so afraid of it?"

"If you understood what was coming, you'd be afraid, Daughter. I was only trying to do what I could to keep our land safe."

"What did they ask of you?"

"They didn't ask anything."

Serena had a hard time thinking that was the case, as she had very little experience with some of these other entities, but what her mother had implied suggested that they had demanded something of her. Though at this point, Serena wasn't sure what that was going to be. "What did they tell you?"

Her mother started to pace again, and for a moment, Serena didn't think that she was going to get any sort of answer from her mother. At this point, maybe it didn't matter. She could feel the palace starting to pulsate, changing, and she wondered if she had to head outside, to add her own connection to it, using the unity, or perhaps it wouldn't even matter. The longer she stayed here, the longer she could feel the palace reacting to whatever Serena had done before, and she could feel that power beginning to flow in a way Serena had never understood.

"All of this was once theirs," her mother finally said. "Is that what you want to hear? All of this was theirs, and they want it back."

That surprised Serena.

If the ancients had that kind of unity and had access to that kind of power, it suggested some reason caused them to change it and had taken them away from that power.

"What do you mean about it being theirs?"

"That is all I know. It was once theirs. They will retake it, especially when you prove how much power remains in this land. That is why you need to stop this."

Could that be what this was about? Power?

"I will not," Serena said.

With that, she strode out of her mother's room, sealed the room shut, and then left the palace. Once she was outside, she looked up along the walls of the palace, feeling it's slowly changing energy of it.

She used a series of different types of essences to press into the stone and began to feel the way it was pulsating in response to her essence, the way it was reacting in some manner as if it had always waited for unity. Even as it did, she could feel some part of it beginning to shift and change, though she wasn't sure if it was anything she was doing or if it was tied to the temple she had activated.

It didn't matter, Serena realized. When she formed the unity essence, and began to push that into the palace, she couldn't feel anything more than what she'd already done. There was the hint of energy and the hint of power, but nothing else that she was going to be able to do. The only thing she could detect was that some aspect of it had already begun to change. And nothing that she added would make a difference.

She had to wait to see what had happened.

She focused on what she could feel of Tessatha, and with a blast of the essence, she was carried up and free from her land, and over to the thorn land. When she reached it, and where she knew Tessatha to be, she hurried inside the small stone cottage that Tessatha had taken over, only to find that it was filled with the fragrance of flowers, the steaming smoke from a teakettle, and the fragrance of the flame in the back hearth. Tessatha was seated at the table, a book opened in front of her and a pen in hand. She looked up as Serena entered.

"I didn't expect to see you so soon," Tessatha said.

Serena smiled tightly. "I should've just called you," she said. "But I've been bothered by something. I don't know what to make of it, and I was hoping that maybe you could help me."

She filled in Tessatha with what she had done and what she had experienced, and as she spoke, Tessatha sat upright, and then closed her book, looking over at Serena with concern etched in her eyes. She said nothing for a long time, as if trying to decide what she was going to do, then finally she nodded slowly.

"I don't know that I have an answer to that, but we were studying something similar before. It was how we had begun to question if unity was necessary. We had speculated that there was a different kind of power that was out there. I can show you something, but I don't know if it's going to be much longer."

"What is it?" Serena asked.

Tessatha offered a hint of a smile.

"Let me just show you."

She got to her feet and followed Serena out of the cottage. Once outside, Tessatha used her essence and then blasted upward, until she was in the air, carried away from the thorn realm.

They didn't go very far. They were along the border of the Borderlands, near Rob's realm, and yet in a place, Serena had never visited before. The land below was barren and rocky, and though it should be connected to essence, and tied to the unity as everything else was, Serena did not have the distinct sense of that unity within it as she would've thought that she should. She came to land, following Tessatha as they did, until they stepped forward into a pile of rubble.

With a wave of her hand, Tessatha forced the rubble upward, and it began to stack. Serena noted a pattern here, and could feel an essence memory that had lingered, and realized that Tessatha was using that memory to create the stone stack. Or perhaps she wasn't even using essence memory. It was hard for Serena to know whether that was the case, or whether she was simply using what she remembered herself. Regardless of what it was, she helped her rebuild the structure until it was formed once again.

It was a small stone cottage that reminded Serena of the one in the thorn realm. Perhaps a bit larger than that one, but the structure was generally the same. She looked over to Tessatha, who was staring at it, her eyes distant, and almost as if she had lost some part of herself.

"What is it?" Serena asked.

"This was once one of our places," Tessatha said softly. "It was lost long ago. I've resisted coming back here, as there are too many memories here, and it's almost better if they remained buried, I suspect."

"Do you think Arowend would have needed to come back here?"

"Arowend came through here once," Tessatha said, looking over at her, before turning her attention back to the cottage. "I could feel his presence. I don't know what he intended to accomplish when he came through here, but I could feel what he did."

The Netheral, Tessatha didn't say. He had come through here, probably looking for some part of himself that he could reunite with others, and perhaps looking for memories that had been lost. All because he had been shattered and destroyed by the essence weapon. Ripped apart in a way that had left him changed and turned into something less than he had been before.

And now...

Now that he had returned, he had not returned. Tessatha had, though.

"There may be some memories that linger here," Tessatha said. "As I said, I haven't been back here, and I don't know if there is anything here that we might be able to find. I've avoided this."

"We don't have to do it, then," Serena said.

She took a deep breath, and when she did, she let it out slowly and then began to pour essence into the stone. She started with the bramble essence, and then shifted, adding one after another, before finally shifting all of them and beginning to blend them into something akin to the unity. When she did, the stone itself began to shift, bubbling with energy. Serena thought it might change the same way the temple changed, drawing upon the unity essence in that manner, but she didn't see anything quite like that. Instead, it was just as if the stone itself started to settle, blending together in a way that looked like it was meant to be.

"If what you're saying is true, then our research is tied to what has happened."

"How is that possible?"

Tessatha shook her head. "I don't know. You would think that some of the difficulties of the past would stay buried in the past, but unfortunately, it seems as if, too often, the past likes to come back to haunt us. At least, it seems that way to me. I'm tired of it haunting me," she said, glancing over to Serena for a moment, and offering a sad sort of smile. "But perhaps allowing me to learn what we had attempted to learn long ago is the benefit. At least, I hope we can find a benefit." She let out another heavy sigh and then turned her attention back to the stone. "Are you ready to go inside?"

Serena wasn't sure that they would find anything. If it had been buried under the rubble, what could they uncover here, anyway? Nothing other than memories that would haunt Tessatha and Arowend.

Serena began to wonder if there were essence memories here that they might be able to find. Even if they were difficult memories, there was the possibility that they would have left some aspect of them behind to make sense of the kind of power that Tessatha and Arowend had once pursued. And there was no doubt in Serena's mind that they had once pursued something, and that those powers were tied to what they were dealing with now. If she could find out what that was and make sense of it, then maybe they'd better understand what was happening and what the Eternal warned them about.

The inside of the cottage was small and cozy. There was a hint of essence inside, though she didn't pull on it, thinking that it was probably better if Tessatha were the one to do that, allowing her to try to reach for the different types of essence that had been here. When she didn't, Tessatha looked over to Serena.

"Everything is lost," she said softly. "I had thought… Well, I suppose it doesn't matter what I had thought."

"You thought something might have survived?"

"Items of power could have survived," she said carefully. "At least, that was the hope. But it seemed as if nothing had remained. Nothing I could use."

Serena wasn't sure if there was anything she could say to help her, so instead, she wandered around the inside of this space. She focused on essence and memories but did not find anything she could puzzle together. Partly because she didn't want to strip away anything that Tessatha might need, and also because there really wasn't much here.

She used a bit of fire, though, casting some light so that she could see everything around her. She noticed a faint glimmering along the ground. When she pointed to it, Tessatha joined her, crouching down.

"What is this?" Serena asked.

"This would be…" She closed her eyes tightly and squeezed her chin for a moment as if trying to decide what she could remember. And then, when she opened her eyes, she looked over at Serena. "I don't remember. There are gaps in my memory, as well. Maybe I'm no better than Arowend."

"I think it's understandable that the both of you have gaps in your memory," Serena said." It's been difficult for you, given everything you've gone through."

Tessatha breathed out heavily. "But we should be able to find something here, I think. This was a place where we studied ancient relics, where we learned what came before."

"How ancient?" Serena asked, tracing her hand along

the surface of the glimmering reflection on the ground in front of her.

"Old, even in our time," Tessatha said.

She seemed startled by her answer, as if she hadn't even known she knew this.

Serena looked down. It would be practically ancient if it was old, even in their time. And it would mean that it was some aspect of the ancients.

Which was exactly what they needed.

"Let's continue our studies, then," Serena said.

Chapter Nine

ROB

Rob flowed along the boundary, looking for evidence of the creature. There was no further sign of him, but he wasn't convinced that they were going to be left alone. He was concerned that the creature would come back for him, attacking.

If it did, he wanted to be ready. It had surprised him that the entity had managed to scratch at the boundary and had done so in a way that Rob had needed to push out with enough strength to help prevent it from shredding his boundary. He was surprised it had managed to do as much as he had. He had thought that his unity essence was enough that he would be able to prevent anything more, but unfortunately…

Unfortunately, it seemed as if he wasn't strong enough for that.

If the heralds came in full, and if they came at him with the same ferocity, would Rob be able to defend against them? He was just one at his level, whatever it was. And as far as he understood, or at least believed, the heralds were all at that same level, which meant they were all incredibly powerful. If they broke through the boundary, they would devastate everything, coming into his land.

Rob had no idea what they were after. Maybe it was just the unity.

Alyssa had warned him that they would come and destroy him, draining his essence. So, maybe that's what they were after. Perhaps Rob, in his urgency to progress, had changed enough things about his realm that he had helped reveal the essence in a way that had not been revealed before. And if that were the case, then it meant that his land had changed because of what he had done and was now a target.

He made his way around the perimeter. Now that he'd progressed to this point, he could travel as fast as he needed. He didn't have any limitation to essence, as it felt as if he were filled with the power of his realm in a way that he had not ever been filled before. He could use that essence, and he could feel the way that it flowed through him, making him all too aware of everything that he possessed, and everything that he could be. By the time he had completed his circuit, he still hadn't found any other sign of the danger.

But he *did* feel something. It was a strangeness. And a familiarity.

Rob stretched out his awareness, using the dragon mind link, and focused on what he could feel of Alyssa, as he was certain that's who was out there. She wasn't inside of his realm, but she was not far, either. It was almost as if she was waiting, hoping to be allowed to come back in.

That's odd.

When he reached her, he could feel some part of her, a presence to her, but then it faded. Rob fortified that connection. As he strained, he began to detect some part of her pushing against him, as if she were trying to push him away.

Rob was stronger than her now, so he didn't have to fear her successfully fighting him off, and so he pushed through that connection until he reached her.

"Why are you fighting me?"

"You can't protect me," she said, and there was exasperation in her voice as she reached through the dragon mind connection, almost as if she realized that she would be able to hold him off, but she also realized that she did not want him to be connected to her. "You need to stop whatever it is that you're doing here."

"What am I doing?" Rob asked. "Other than trying to protect everything."

She laughed.

"Your people need more than what you can do, Guardian."

Even as she said it, though, Rob began to feel some part of her coming closer. It was as if her essence were drifting across the boundary.

He didn't hold her back, as he didn't fear Alyssa or any of the others that were with her. Not because they couldn't cause damage—they absolutely could—but because he had hoped he could draw them into fighting alongside him.

He wasn't sure if she would agree to it, given how she'd proven that she was willing to run, but he also felt as if he wanted to try to reach her in some manner. If he could find a way to get through to her, he hoped there would be some way to have more help.

"I can feel you were coming toward me," Rob said.

Alyssa was quiet for a moment, though the power radiated from her as she drifted in his direction. As she headed toward him, he could feel her and how she was drawing power. It was almost as if she wanted to make sure that he was fully aware of everything she was doing, though that was a strange awareness for him, too.

By the time she neared, it seemed as if a cloud of debris had followed her. As Rob suspected, she wasn't quite a storm cloud; her connection was far greater than just a storm cloud. She was something more. The others with her were the same. Whatever it was, they were powerful.

Alyssa stepped forward, moving out of the power cloud, and revealing herself. She looked tired. That was new. Every other time that Rob had seen her, she had looked alert and bright-eyed and had seemed almost as if she were struggling with whatever it was that they had been dealing with.

"Why did you call me?" she asked.

"What makes you think I called you? Maybe you're the one who called to me."

Energy crackled around her, and it was a series of power, almost as if she were attempting to use something akin to the unity but wasn't quite strong enough. Perhaps if she had more experience, she'd be able to do that, but at this point, it didn't seem as if she could use it the same way that Rob could.

He would have to help her.

That realization struck him, as he hadn't considered the possibility that he would need to help Alyssa and her people, but he should have thought about that. They weren't of his realm, though, they had obviously been a part of this battle before, and he would need every ally he had, assuming they were willing to fight alongside him. Rob didn't know if Alyssa and the others were going to fight, as any time that it had come down to a battle, at least a battle directly against the Eternal—which meant any battle against one of the heralds—she had not been interested.

"Have you ever seen a creature with wings and a beak that looks something like a human?" Rob asked, sending a vision through the dragon's mind connection to her.

As soon as he did, Alyssa reacted, jerking back, and the energy that she was holding onto crackled with even more ferocity. It was almost as if she were trying to defend herself against the creature, even though it wasn't even there.

"I guess that answers that," Rob said.

"Where did you see it?"

"Along the border," he said. "It came, decided to taunt me, and then departed."

"We call them the subherald," she said. "We aren't sure what they're called, but they come before the heralds. At least, they have before. They're skilled at destroying, and they've ripped through our protections."

Rob thought about what the subherald attempted to

do to his barrier, and how it had very nearly succeeded. "How powerful are they?"

"Not as powerful as the heralds, if that's your concern, but there are *more* of them."

"There was only one."

"Only one that you saw," she said.

Rob frowned. *Could there have been more?*

There was only one attack at the boundary, but there was the possibility that others were beyond. Maybe they were trying to decide whether they'd be able to attack him and if they could break through the boundary. But, if they were trying to break through the boundary, why would they not have sent more of the subheralds against him?

"If there were more, then why wouldn't they have attacked?"

"Who's to say? What did the subherald tell you?"

"That the heralds are coming. Then again, the Eternal has said the same thing."

Alyssa frowned for a moment, and the power that she was holding onto continued to crackle through her as if she were trying to radiate some of that energy outward from her. It burst with a bit of overwhelming energy, and then retreated, drawn back into whatever it was that she used as a reportable realm.

"You're making a mistake here. Drawing enemies to you is dangerous."

"I'm not trying to draw enemies to me, but they are coming nonetheless."

"I'd be less concerned about the heralds and more concerned about who they represent."

Rob hovered before Alyssa. He had been questioning the Eternal, trying to make sense of all that power, and hoping that he might be able to find something more to what had happened, but had not been able to do so.

The Eternal feared the other entity.

And fear was a powerful motivator, Rob knew. Fear had certainly motivated plenty of people while he had been progressing. It motivated *him* to progress.

"As far as I can tell, nobody knows what they represent."

"I don't either," Alyssa said, "if that's what you're trying to get at. All I know is that there is something greater than the Eternal, and greater than the heralds, that we cannot counter. We may not be able to *ever* counter."

She looked behind her, and for a moment, he could feel the energy crackling from her to the others, as if the portable realms were more than just a singular realm, and instead were something of a unified entity. And maybe that was what they were. Rob simply did not know if they were all bonded together in some way. They certainly traveled together. Rob had seen Alyssa alone, but she almost always traveled with the others.

The portable realms might be useful in the future if it came down to fighting whatever this other entity was. Then again, Rob suspected that he was going to need every bit of power that he possessed and would need to find some way to counter the other entities, but he hadn't yet done so.

"Have you thought about progressing?" Rob asked.

Alyssa turned to him, and there was a bright look of

amusement that shone on her face. "Have we considered progressing? It's all that we think about. It's the only way that we're going to do anything more against this power, and we know that. And yet there is you, dancing through your realm, still connected to your land, and able to do… Well, whatever it is that you can do."

"I can help," Rob said.

She smiled at him slightly. "You really think that your understanding of what it means for you to progress is going to be applicable to what it means for us to progress?"

"Progression is similar," Rob said. "Regardless of the type of essence, regardless of how you reach it, I suspect there is a way to help you."

But then again, Rob hadn't even helped any of the other dragon blood in his realm progress from where they were to where he was. He had to wonder if perhaps he could bring Alyssa to the nexus, but if he were to do that, there was no guarantee that it was going to be enough strength or power or the right kind of essence for her to blend what she had.

Alyssa just watched him. Finally, she smiled again. "You see the problem, don't you? You have access to something in your land we do not have."

"Could you?"

"I don't know," she began. "I told you that they came and destroyed it. That's what they're after, after all. Well, that and essence. They came in, ripped away what we had, and left us with nothing."

Rob thought about what would happen if his realm were to face the same thing, and how it might feel. They had quite a bit of essence in his realm, and yet, if it were stripped away, how would he feel about that?

Rob knew how he would feel. He would be angry.

"There was a secret in my land," Rob began carefully. "An ancient power. It was called the nexus, though I'm not sure what the ancients would've called it. It was a place where the powers were all blended together. Once I reached it, I was able to blend my own essences together. It's possible that if you were to go there—"

"Again, it's your realm, not mine." She waved her hand backward, toward her portable realm. "I don't think that there's going be the same technique for us. I do appreciate your interest in helping, though," she said with a smile. "But, we have to find our own means of progressing. We will."

"Did you have any records of it?"

"Records?" Alyssa asked, and there was real anger in her voice. "Of course, we *had* records. But that's what they do. They come in and destroy. They come in and strip away all that we were before. They come in and take."

Rob realized they didn't want the others to have any knowledge of progression.

But why would that be? Was it fear?

The heralds had obviously progressed, and the others that served the heralds had progressed, so it seemed to Rob that plenty of these entities had power and were permitted to continue to gain it. But there had to be something more to it. The problem was Rob didn't know what that would entail. If they came to lands, stripped essence, and then destroyed records…

It meant that whatever they had done wasn't permanent otherwise.

"Where is your land?"

Alyssa looked behind her. She was quiet for a long moment, then called the portable realm toward her, floating back on top of it. She stood there for a long moment, and Rob had a distinct sense of the energy she filled with, flowing through the realm and out from her. "It's here."

"It's more than just there," Rob said. "Where did you originally come from? I think that's going to be the key."

"I told you. My land was lost. There is nothing left of it. Nothing left for us."

Rob wanted to reassure her, but he wasn't sure either. Instead, he thought that he could try to help.

"I wonder if there might still be something there," he said. "I don't know what it is, but I can't help but wonder if perhaps there might still be a memory there, and if you can find that memory, you might be able to find answers."

He'd dealt with enough essence memories that he had to believe that it was possible. But it seemed improbable, especially given what she claimed. Still, Rob wasn't going to believe that there was no hope until he had a chance to help her.

"I told you; my land was lost."

"But where was it?"

Alyssa shook her head. "You can be quite stubborn, can't you?"

"Sometimes I have to be," Rob said.

"If I show you, what do you think you're going to do?

Go and find a barren land and then have me prove to you just how little we can be? I told you what happened, and how little we have left, so…"

"You've proven to me that your land was lost, but you haven't proven anything more. We don't know that there aren't memories still there."

"They stripped the essence away," she said. "There is nothing left."

"But did they also destroy all of your records?"

"So?"

"They wouldn't do that if there wasn't some way to use that essence. They might've stripped away the essence then, but what if some remain? What if *enough* of it remains that you can use it?"

It was hard for Rob not to be excited about the possibility, partly because he wanted to try to help her, but also because if he helped her, he might gain real allies.

"Essence doesn't work like that," she said.

"I think I've learned one thing about essence: it is not at all like I think it should be. If you show me, I will see if there's anything I can do to help. But I'm going to need you to help me understand how to make a portable realm first."

Alyssa looked behind her, and then she turned her attention back to him. "Fine. I suppose this doesn't hurt anything. Other than your pride when you fail. But are you sure you want to be away from your people?"

"My boundary is safe."

At least, it was safe for now. He wasn't sure how long it would stay that way, but he was determined to keep it that way. And he would make it even safer by helping Alyssa.

"Should we go?" Rob asked.

Alyssa wrapped herself in her portable realm, and there was a moment where he felt power crackling, and it took him a moment to realize it was what she was doing. She was showing him how to do the same thing. The realm was not complicated. He drew upon the unity, calling it to him, and then sealed it off.

He connected to Serena for a moment. "I'm going to see something. I may be distant for a little while."

There was a brief surge through the conduit as if Serena were giving him an acknowledgment, but then it went silent.

With that, he followed Alyssa and her people, traveling beyond his boundary.

Chapter Ten

SERENA

Serena stared at the relic, trying to make sense of it. It was strangely shaped, made of metal, and had written that she could not read. She had to get it out of the ground, as she hadn't figured out anything about it yet. The only thing that she was able to determine was that it had a sense of power buried within the relic, something that seemed to be tied to the unity essence, though increasingly, Serena wasn't sure if what it was tied to be her type of unity or if it was tied, Rob. As she focused on the unity and the way she blended the essences together, she found that it didn't mingle quite as well as she thought it needed to do for the essence to flow into the strange cylindrical relic.

She sat back, looking at it while seated at the table. The air smelled of the smoke that Tessatha had lit in the hearth, which Serena found to be a bit strange given that she could just use fire, but there was something quite cozy about a natural type of fire here. Perhaps that's why she had done it. Having something more natural than what they usually did felt almost as if they were able to feel like they didn't have to depend upon their essence for them to do everything.

She breathed out and focused again on bundling the essences together the way she had been doing for quite some time. Ever since they had dug out the relics, Serena had been trying to make sense of them and thinking that there might be some way for her to understand if there was anything more within them that she could use. Unfortunately, even as she had been attempting to do so, she hadn't found anything more.

"I think there is a contour here we should examine further," the librarian said, looking down upon the relic.

She had manifested him here, though it was very easy for him to manifest now, to the point where she wasn't even sure if she had much control over where and when he manifested. She summoned him when she became concerned about what she had found about the relic, and wondered if there was going to be anything she could uncover about it, without any help. Tessatha was off looking at some of the other sites she and Arowend had once occupied, to the point where she had left Serena alone for quite some time. Serena had been trying to reach Rob, but he'd gone silent. She thought he was safe, as she still had a vague awareness of him, but she wasn't quite sure what he'd done and where he was. As far as she could tell, he didn't seem to be in the realm any longer.

Why would that be the case, though? Where would Rob have gone?

"What sort of contour do you think you have uncovered? I've been looking at this thing for the better part of the last day and haven't uncovered anything about it."

"It's more in the way that the markings seem to be made," the librarian said and took a seat across from her. He was a manifestation, but he was solidly manifested.

Serena wasn't sure if he was the primary manifestation, or if this was one of his secondary manifestations. She suspected that he was spread throughout the realms, working in many of the different libraries to determine what else they might find. The librarian had been searching and testing different relics, ancient markings, and writings while trying to uncover more information about the ancients. So far, she had not found anything that had helped Serena with her belief that unity was key to all of this.

"If you look at the tracings here, you can see how the power seems to flow in this direction," he said. "But once you begin to activate it with your unity essence, that power begins to shift, spiraling this way," he said, tracing his finger along the inside of the relic.

She felt it; the way the power flowed through it had changed, but it had done so in a way Serena wasn't quite certain that she could mimic. That was what she was trying to do, after all. She'd wanted to know if she could turn the power into something familiar to her.

So far, the answer to that question was *no*. There was nothing she could do to that power, or to modify it, that would help her understand whether she could make it more like the ancients had made their relics. The markings seemed to be the key to them, but every time that she tried to replicate it, she found that she could not do nearly what the ancients had done, despite feeling as if she had a great comprehension of what they were doing, and perhaps even how they were doing it.

"Have you uncovered anything more about the writing style?"

That was something that the librarian had been studying, and in the time that he had been there, Serena had made sure that she stayed linked to him and his memories so that she could gain access to anything he might uncover. She didn't think that he was holding out on her, but given that it was a manifestation, and had considerable power, Serena didn't even know if what he could do would be replicable.

"There are aspects in some of the ancient writings that help me understand what they have done, but unfortunately, there are aspects that I cannot quite follow. This style is quite different from what we've seen in many buildings. I would've said that the buildings were old, but everything I've seen suggests that while they are old, they are not nearly as old as this."

He tapped on the relic, and then there was a surge of essence from him. He was connected to power, and increasingly, it seemed as if some part of him had begun to shift as if he were taking on aspects of the unity essence. That didn't seem quite as strange now as it once had, especially as she had seen the temples and the palace, beginning to shift with the connection to that unity essence. Still, she suspected that the librarian had once been of a singular type of essence, and the sudden change, or not so sudden, she realized, left her wondering if what Rob had done had somehow changed him in dangerous ways.

Unless he had always been part of this unity essence, Serena realized.

She didn't really know all that much about it. She thought that she understood the age of the librarian and that he had been around during Tessatha's time, or perhaps maybe somewhat earlier than that, but she wasn't sure if that was even accurate. There were gaps in his memory, much like there were gaps in Arowend's memory, and within those who had become manifestations of the essence. All struggled to a certain degree, losing some part of their essence. Unless they were intentional about how they manifested, she wondered if such a thing would always be the case.

"We need to understand all of this better," she said to him. "It seems to be all tied to the unity, leaving me thinking that this is important."

"Well, of course, it's important," the librarian said, and he grabbed the relic from her, pulling it closer to him. It always left her marveling when he could do that, as he was just a manifestation; however, he was manifested potently. "If you feel the power here, there's an obvious purpose behind this, and it traces through in a way that leaves me suspecting that there was once something more to it, only…" He looked up at her and locked eyes for a moment, before turning his attention back down. When he did, there was a surge through the link between the two of them that left Serena feeling the memories that he was shuffling through as he tried to make sense of what this was and what it might be able to do. "I feel as if I have seen this before, Mistress."

Serena sat upright. That was new information. "How?"

"I don't recall," he said, and when he looked up at her again, his eyes were brimming with a bit of irritation. Most of the time, the librarian was fairly neutral and seemed as if he wanted to be simply subservient, but the only times that she had seen the irritation in his gaze was tied to when he felt as if he were letting her down, though Serena didn't think that he was letting her down, maybe he felt that way. "There's a familiarity when I look at this, and I begin to question if I've seen it before."

Serena watched him for a moment. "What do you remember about yourself?"

The librarian stared at the relic for a long moment. "I don't think that's relevant, Mistress."

Serena smiled, though the librarian still hadn't looked up, so he didn't see it. "And I think that it's relevant. You're a manifestation of the essence, no different than Arowend," she hurriedly added, feeling as if she needed to take away some of the stings of that comment, though she wasn't sure if it even stung him. "And there are certain things that you have experienced and know that I'm not even sure we can even understand. When you're in the palace, I thought that perhaps you were just tied to the palace archive, but seeing as how you've been changing, I'm starting to question if perhaps my understanding of you, and what you experienced before, might've been mistaken."

The essence within him seemed to flutter for just a

moment, long enough that Serena knew she was right in the question she had about it. She smiled to herself. She didn't feel as if she needed to question him too much, or too hard, but at the same time, she also felt as if he needed to try to find a way to answer these questions, and they needed to understand better what they were dealing with.

"You don't have to feel as if you need to withhold anything from me," she went on. "We need everything that you know."

He pulled the relic closer to him and began tracing his hand along its curved rim. It started to glow slightly, as if he were activating some of the symbols within it, but Serena recognized that he was simply pouring some fire essence out of himself and into the relic, focusing on fire more than anything else. Still, despite using only fire, Serena could feel some aspect of the unity flowing within him. She wasn't sure if it was coming from her, as she seemed to be the one that was connected to the librarian, or whether this was tied to something else, but she also didn't think it even mattered. At this point, the only thing that really mattered was that she could feel that.

"There are too many things I don't know," the librarian said. "When you woke me before, I felt... Well, I felt as if I were serving in the way that I was supposed to serve. Does that make any sort of sense?"

"It does," Serena said. "You were trapped inside the library of the palace. And the palace was mounted to fire, so I thought you were only tied to fire, but with everything I have seen lately, I'm starting to wonder if you were bound to something more." She nodded her head toward the relic. "I have begun to activate essence all around these realms, and I realized that unity seems to be a part of things for far longer than we've realized. That seems… Well, it seemed significant to me," she went on. "And the more that I begin to learn, the more that I have uncovered about it, the more that I start to wonder if the essences that were bound inside of some of these older structures, much like the palace, were more complicated than I realized."

It didn't make that much sense to her, but she increasingly felt there had to be something more than what she had already learned. The palace had seemed to be tied to fire, but it also was tied to these others in a way that she wasn't even sure she fully understood. Yet, she felt as if she needed to learn so that she could master that essence and see if there was something that connected them to the unity tower that had simply appeared.

The unity tower and the nexus, which Serena also thought was significant.

"I have begun to speculate on that," the librarian said, and when he looked up at her, Serena saw that his eyes were blazing with a bit of fire within them. "As my memories seem to be tied primarily to the palace, but over time, I feel as if there is something more that has been awoken inside of me. I don't know if it is tied to what you have done, or if there is perhaps something more I am supposed to find, but I do feel as if there is something here that I can uncover." He looked out into the relic, then pressed his hands deep into it.

Serena didn't think that she would be able to do the same thing, as the relic was not wide enough for her to stop her hand from it. But she might be able to manifest some part of herself into it, which she suspected the librarian had done.

"As everything begins to change, I feel some part of myself shifting. As if I'm somehow more whole, but I don't understand why that would be. I suspect that answers will come in learning the languages and about these ancients, as it seems they are all interconnected."

Serena nodded. "As far as I can tell, everything like that is interconnected, and that's part of the reason that we need to master these essences. Rob has uncovered something, but it's not just what Rob uncovered. It's what Tessatha and Arowend have been doing before that. They were researching this in their era, enough so that they recognized there was a key to the blended essence, but even then, the ancients were... Well, ancient. So whatever else we are dealing with, it is incredibly old, and that, I suspect, is what the heralds are after."

Not just the heralds, Serena suspected. It was whatever the heralds served. That was the power that they were after.

Maybe it was simply pure essence. Increasingly, Serena believed that by awakening the unity, she was changing things into a purer form, bridging it back into what others could use. And if that were the case, then perhaps that was all she needed to know about it, because pure essence was incredibly valuable. If others had pure essence, they could continue to progress, but...

They could only reach the dragon's mind with pure essence.

Anything beyond that required something else.

But what she had seen so far didn't strike her as a

limit. She wasn't entirely sure what that was about, but she felt the answers were right before her, perhaps buried somewhere.

And it all came down to trying to find answers that were lost to time. Unfortunately, it also came down to doing what Rob had suggested they do and tracking through the essence memories throughout the realm. Those essence memories trapped information and knowledge they had lost, finally allowing them to understand how to master aspects of this essence.

She looked over to the relic. There had to be more like it.

The door opened, and Serena looked over.

Tessatha strode in, glanced at the librarian, bowed her head politely to him, and then took a seat across from Serena, sitting next to the librarian. Arowend joined her only a moment later, but he remained standing, as he seemed a little uncomfortable, primarily around Serena. He had been like that ever since he started regaining some of his memories, which Serena appreciated. If he had been unconcerned about what he'd done when he had been another, Serena wasn't sure that she could spend any time around him, but in this form, as Arowend, she felt …

It was easier for her to rationalize it that way, thinking about him as Arowend, rather than the Netheral.

"We have found more relics," she said, dropping her bag on the table. "Actually, Arowend found more relics. His memory of them is a bit better than mine. Then again, he was always the relic hunter back when he was…"

Tessatha flushed slightly, and she looked over to Arowend, with a look in her eyes that seemed to be begging him for forgiveness.

He smiled at her, and there was warmth in those eyes. "What did you find?"

"Well, there was a series of different places he brought me. After we came here and rebuilt this structure," she said, waving her hand around her, "I decided to see if there might be other places. Most of them were in the same form as this one, but it really does take very little effort to rebuild it, so we can at least examine the inside of it. Over time, I think that we might be able to rebuild quite a few of these different structures."

The implication struck Serena. If they were to rebuild some of these ancient ruins, they might be able to find out more about what the ancients had done, and the purpose behind some of those ruins.

Many of them seemed as if they were lost, but they really weren't. The memory was there, and they had a way of mingling was essences, blending them together in a useful form. It was little more than a wave of her hand to rebuild some of these structures and form them once again.

"And?"

"And there are many other relics like this," Arowend said, turning away from where he was standing near the wall, and nodding toward the relic on the table. "Perhaps not quite like that, but each seems to have a different purpose. Unfortunately, I'm not able to determine the purpose behind it. Maybe Rob could."

There was a hint of irritation in his words, though

Serena wasn't sure if it was pointed at Rob, or if it was pointed at the fact that Arowend couldn't identify the key. Maybe a little bit of both. She didn't get the sense that Arowend was all that disappointed that he hadn't been able to take on the unity essence. Rob had made it clear that Arowend had been there when he had progressed and had been the one who had urged Rob to do whatever was necessary for him to become… Well, whatever it was that Rob had become.

"So, we have quite a few different ancient relics, no idea what they do, but let me guess. They all seem to be tied to the unity?"

"As far as I can tell," Tessatha said, looking over to Arowend as she spoke. "I don't remember feeling that way before."

"I don't know that we had the full unity before," Arowend said. "Though I could be mistaken. I don't remember things as well as I need to. But Rob added water. That was something we weren't considering."

"Maybe there are other essences that we still haven't found," Serena offered.

"Probably," Arowend said, "but I don't know if that matters for the unity of this realm. It seems this realm is tied to the forms of the essence we have already uncovered, including the water surrounding it. And yet, I still feel like there are parts of what we have been doing and what we have been finding that don't make complete sense to me. I feel like we are so close to that understanding, but all we need to do is keep digging…"

Now Serena thought that she understood his frustration.

It was tied to feeling like he had overlooked something when he was active. That was something that Serena, as a scholar, completely understood. She had felt that way before and recognized that Tessatha and Arowend had studied far more than Serena had. Far more than Rob had. And yet, Serena and Rob had uncovered things they had not managed to do.

Why now?

Serena didn't have the answer to that and wasn't even sure it mattered. Not at this point. The only thing that mattered was that they continued digging for those answers. And they needed Tessatha and Arowend to help with it. But they also need the librarian, in whatever form he had, to keep looking. They needed information and to know more than what they had done so far.

"Why don't we go and look at these other relics," she said. "Maybe we can find something useful."

"I would like to come, Mistress," the librarian said.

"I think you should," Serena said. And for Tessatha and Arowend's benefit, she added, "Because you have begun to change. Your essence has begun to change. And all of that is probably tied to what's happening now. It's unity, and we need to understand it. And if there's anybody who might be able to help us understand, it's somebody who is tied to it in ways that we are not quite."

Tessatha focused on the librarian, and there was a flickering of the essence as she tried to test the librarian. Serena wasn't entirely sure what she did, only that she could feel the way the power flashed out from her and toward the librarian, before dissipating altogether.

She frowned, her brow furrowing, but she said nothing.

"Should we go?" Serena asked.

"You should go," Arowend said. "I need to try to reach Rob."

"I don't think he's in any danger," Serena said.

"I can feel that he's grown distant," Arowend said. "And distance makes me worry."

She frowned again. "Worry?"

What was there to worry about? If there were something to worry about, she would've felt it from her Rob, but she had not. Maybe there was more to it than she realized. And if that were the case, then why had Rob not sent out some sort of alert to her?

Unless he couldn't.

"Not for his safety, but for what he's found. Don't worry. I'll do that for both of us."

Serena wasn't sure that she could trust Arowend—the Netheral—to worry on her behalf, but at the same time, she knew that she needed to go with Tessatha to explore these other relics. It was time for her to trust a little bit, regardless of how difficult it might be.

She nodded.

She followed Tessatha, and the librarian came with her, staying manifested, and they took to the sky, chasing down ancient relics. Serena couldn't shake the comment that Arowend had made about Rob, nor could she shake the hint of worry she now had for him, leaving her to wonder if perhaps something more had taken place that she still didn't understand. And if so, maybe she needed to take action on his behalf.

But what could she do to help Rob? She didn't have Rob's ability, and she certainly didn't have his strength. The only thing she had was…

My mind.

Unless she were to progress.

And as she focused on the unity, she felt all around her, Serena knew she needed to progress. If she didn't, she wasn't sure she would be able to understand what was happening around them fully. She felt an urgency to progress for the first time in a long time. Maybe she was becoming more like Rob.

Chapter Eleven

ROB

The air whistled around Rob as he chased Alyssa, moving quickly. He had the power that he had bound behind and around him. It seemed to link him to his own realm, but there was something quite artificial about it. Rob could feel that artificial nature that left him thinking it was not quite right. He didn't know what it was, only that some part of that bound energy was unusual.

It didn't separate quite the same way as it would've otherwise, so in that regard, Rob thought he was safer by having this power linked to him in the way it did. He had been focusing on it, letting that energy stay connected to him, while also starting to feel some other aspect of it surging beneath him. He was still dragon blood, or whatever it was that he now was given that he had bound to the unity and had that essence that flowed out and around him in a way that created almost a blanket of power that surged. He could draw upon that blanket and felt that energy tied to him.

Not surprisingly, it was not nearly as potent as it would've been, had he been in his realm. He had brought a portion of it, but not nearly enough for him to feel as if he could defend himself the way he once would have.

Would the conduit make a difference?

He had used that when he needed to ensure he had access to true strength. It was a way of linking to something else—something more.

Rob was hesitant to open that conduit any more than he already had, not wanting Serena to know he was doing this. He had warned her that he was leaving, but he hadn't quite told her where he was going or what he was doing. And all of that felt a little deceptive to him, even though he was not trying to keep anything from her. At least, not really. Still, as he chased Alyssa beyond the borders of his own realm, beyond where he had felt his power, Rob couldn't help but feel as if some part of him was left behind.

But this is necessary.

That was what he kept telling himself as he flowed over the water. Even the water essence was different, the color of it darker, deeper, as if he had reached some different part of the ocean, he had never seen before. There was no sign of Oro's essence, the same kind of essence that Rob was connected to, though there was essence down below. As far as Rob could tell, none of the sea monsters that he knew existed in this part of the world, had chased them. Either they weren't aware of their presence, or they simply decided not to attack. Still, Rob did not want to take too much time doing this, not wanting to give any of these others a chance to chase him down, and attack. His ability to defend himself would be limited compared to what it would've been had he been in his realm.

A part of him remained a little on edge, worried that perhaps Alyssa and the others were leading him into a trap. He kept questioning himself. What did he really know about Alyssa and her friends? Not much. Certainly not enough to know whether they would try to betray him. He didn't think that was the case, but there was the possibility that they were interested in bringing him away, tearing him free from his realm, where he couldn't defend himself nearly as powerfully as he had before.

But if that were the case, then why would they have taught him about making his own miniature realm? This gave him a connection to unity and also enough power to defend himself for a little while. Perhaps long enough to escape.

So, he chased.

In the distance, he noticed a massive, darkened form of land.

He slowed, watching for a moment as he tested whether there was any sign of essence within it. He couldn't determine anything, but perhaps he was just too far away. The others had slowed, and he wondered if there was something more to it than what he had already felt. So far, he couldn't tell. By the time he caught up to Alyssa, who had started to slow down so he could catch up, the others had slowed as well, creating a bit of a ring around the outer edge of this land.

"Here?" Rob asked, glancing over to Alyssa.

There was no emotion on her face, not as he

would've expected if this was her land and her realm that had been stripped away. It was barren rock below, little more than black and brown emptiness as if every bit of it had been stolen. He couldn't imagine how he would feel if this was his realm. Though he had long struggled to feel as if some part of the realm was home, he had begun to claim all of it for himself, making it so that Rob felt as if everything was his. And if something had happened to him, he would not have dealt with it nearly as calmly as Alyssa obviously did.

"This is not mine. This is Terrence and Marlena's realm."

She pointed to a pair of people who were far off to his left. As Rob looked over to them, he noticed that Terrence, an older man with graying hair and a scar on one cheek, was staring, tears streaming from his eyes. Marlena was quiet, almost somber, but there was an edge to her. Rob had never paid much attention to either of them, only knowing them as members of whatever it was that Alyssa was doing, but now he could feel something from them. Perhaps he should have taken the time to know them, as he felt that might be key to what was happening here.

"So, you see? There is nothing. You believe that there might be something here, but—"

Rob ignored her as he burst forward.

There might not be anything obvious, but he had a hard time thinking there would be nothing. What they had suggested about the heralds and how they had stripped away not only power, but knowledge left Rob feeling as if there had to be some other aspect that remained. Maybe it wouldn't be obvious, but if it was there, he would help them find it, and he would help them see what they might be able to do.

If anything.

Rob didn't know if there would be anything he could do or help them with, but he felt as if there had to be something. By the time he reached the outskirts of the land, he had pressed over the water and then...

Then there was a strange emptiness.

It came from the lack of essence. It was quite stark. Had he not had the unity with him, he wasn't sure that he would have been able to withstand that sense, and he wasn't sure how he would've responded to it. It all felt overwhelming to him in a certain regard, as the emptiness here left him quite aware of just what should be here but was not.

Only Rob couldn't help but feel as if there was *something*. It wasn't obvious to him, but it was deep. He began to test, though he wasn't even sure how he was going to test, only that he felt as if there was something that he needed to try to do. He started to probe with his essence, letting it strain out from him, attempting to push downward, thinking that there was something within that essence that he might uncover, and perhaps may even be able to free. As he continued to probe, he started to recognize that something deep beneath the surface was reacting to him.

It was reacting to unity.

"What are you doing?" Alyssa asked, joining him. She was looking around, her eyes narrowed.

"I can feel the essence," Rob said. "It's buried, but it's there. If you focus, you can feel it."

"There isn't anything here," she said." This land has been stripped. That is what they do. They harvest. They are parasites. They steal and drain it."

"Essence can't be removed completely," Rob said. He believed that the essence here was hiding, in a certain regard. "They might have taken some of it, but I doubt they took all of it. And if you can find it, and reconnect to it…"

"It won't matter," Alyssa said. She nodded to Terrence and Marlena, both of whom were still at the edge of the boundary of their realm. "They would have felt it."

"Would they have?" Rob asked softly. "I can only feel it because of the unity. Perhaps you can't feel it; they can feel it because you have not yet found it. But if you do…"

He wasn't even sure what would happen if they could find that. Maybe they could all understand the power in a way they hadn't before, and maybe they could become something more. Maybe they could draw essence in a way that they hadn't before.

Or maybe none of it would make a difference.

The heralds were too strong, and this other entity they served was equally strong.

Rob moved over the land. It wasn't nearly as massive as he first thought. It was a large island, but from what he could tell, it seemed situated at the edge of a series of islands. Perhaps that was the different type of realm that Alyssa came from. He focused on it, yet as he swept over it, he did not find any sign of unity. Maybe there was none. But he believed that there had to be something here.

They moved on. Rob took the lead now, and Alyssa ignored his attempt at talking to her. He could feel something, though he wasn't sure what it was. Maybe it was just the fact that he recognized that there were other islands out here, and he found them. They stopped at several others, each carrying the same buried sense of essence, but when he said something to Alyssa, she reacted the same way she had before, either disbelieving or simply choosing not to believe. Either way, Rob thought it was the wrong reaction, as he could feel something here and thought that mattered.

"You have to show me where your land was," Rob said.

"Why?" Alyssa asked as they floated above the water.

They were in the middle of several different islands, and so far, Rob had continued to feel the vague and faint form of essence, but nothing that could be pulled out and used, despite what Rob thought he could feel from it. He wondered if it was tied to the unity, or maybe something was buried deeper, something unreachable.

"What do you think you'll do with my realm?"

"Perhaps there'll be an answer there. Isn't that what you want?"

"What I want doesn't matter," she said. "What I want is for my land to have never suffered like this. What I want is for..." She shook her head, and she stared off into the distance.

Rob followed the direction of her gaze, and he saw a

massive stretch of land. It was larger than many of the others. Quite a bit larger.

"What happened to the others from your land?"

Alyssa was quiet. "I told you."

"No. You told me what happened with the heralds, and how they came for power—essence. You haven't told me about your people."

"Most of them didn't escape. Those that did... we haven't seen in a long time."

He drifted toward the land but didn't move as fast as he had been, as he didn't want to go any faster than Alyssa was willing to travel. He appreciated her staying with him, as he thought she needed to stay with him. By the time they reached it, he had begun to feel some energy bubbling from within it, but it was more than just that energy that he was able to feel. There was something else to it. Some bit of lost danger.

As soon as he reached the outskirts of it, he began to probe, focusing on the essence that he had felt within some of the other places. As before, Rob recognized that there was buried essence. This time, it felt as if there was much more essence than there'd been before.

Rather than trying to explain it to Alyssa, he made a connection between them. He had not done that with her all that often, as he had been hesitant to open himself freely to her, as he didn't know how she was going to respond to it. In this case, though, he could feel a jerk from her, as if she were worried, he might use the power to do something with it.

"Just feel it," he said.

The resistance within her began to fade, though he

did so slowly. He continued to focus, drawing upon what he could feel from her, and he pushed through the energy he detected, the hint of the essence that was buried. There was power there, and he wanted her to know what he felt, as he thought it was essential for her to do so. Increasingly, Rob could feel that power bubbling deep, and yet...

And yet it was so buried that he wasn't sure that he would be able to do much with it. It was too difficult to have access, at least for him.

Because it wasn't *his* essence, he was aware of that. There was a familiarity to it, though even as he focused on it, Rob couldn't tell what kind of essence it was. Given that it was buried as deeply as it was, there didn't seem to be the same conductivity as there might have been otherwise. By holding onto it through the unity, Rob recognized it as essence only, but that essence didn't react to him in any sort of familiar way.

"It's there," she said softly.

"I told you that it was," Rob said.

"It's so—"

Alyssa's essence suddenly surged, and a power bubble built around her.

Rob felt others near him doing the same thing, and he turned, spinning in place as he reacted, trying to make sense of what was happening. The suddenness of their reaction suggested that they were in danger, or at least perceived that they were, but Rob didn't see anything.

Until he did.

Creatures were coming toward them.

That was the only way that he could describe it. And

Rob had seen creatures like that before. They had wings, arms, and legs like a human, a strangely birdlike head with a massive beak. And they were shrieking. Rob hadn't been aware of it before, but now that he noticed it, and heard that shrieking, he couldn't help but feel the power they radiated.

The subheralds were coming.

He turned to Alyssa, but she had the others had already burst away.

"Where are you going?"

Alyssa reacted, answering him quickly, but with urgency. "We cannot do anything here. We need to go."

"We can say. We can fight. We need to know what is here."

"Not here," she said. There was panic in her voice.

He was separated from his essence, cut off from everything that he knew, and he couldn't tell if there was going to be any way for him to able to react. Not yet.

But he also needed to know. So, he hesitated.

As the subheralds got closer, he braced. There were three of them and given what he had experienced with these subherald before, Rob thought he could handle three.

He was a dragon blood bound to the unity.

And he had managed to deal with the herald, so Rob thought this was within his potential.

Then two more. He hadn't even seen them.

Power began to build around him. At first, the power was strong, but then it began to rise with an intensity that Rob tried to push outward with. He had access to the unity through his portable realm, but even as he tried to draw upon that essence, he could tell that there were limits to the power that he was going to be able to pull upon. He attempted to keep pushing, bulging outward as he thought he might have to fight through this, but he wasn't sure if he could draw upon the necessary power to do what he needed.

He glanced behind him; the others had already disappeared, turning, and leaving. Then the subheralds had him surrounded.

They circled, wings fluttering, and power was building from them. Rob could feel that energy coming off them, and he wondered if he might be able to blast his way out. It would be difficult.

But he had to try.

He used the connection to the unity, targeting the nearest of the subheralds, and sent a burst of power at it. When he did, he felt resistance, and then…

Then the power pushed back upon him.

His unity connection was limited. He had power, but Rob didn't have *enough* power. He was in their realm, and they were connected to power in ways he was not. And that, more than anything else, put him in danger.

He had to fight, but could he do so?

They had him surrounded, and they had pinched his power inward and had proven that they knew how to limit him in ways that he did not know how to counter. He thought that he could go upward, and when he tried, they simply flew up with him.

What choice did Rob have, then?

He wasn't helpless. He had different techniques, unity, and perhaps more than that, he had access to the conduit. He had Serena. He had the other dragon's blood.

He wasn't going to be helpless here.

And so, he braced himself for a battle unlike any that he had ever faced.

Chapter Twelve

SERENA

Serena's arms were full of the relics that they had gathered. Most of them reminded her of the relic they had in Tessatha's home, but not all of them were. Some of them were larger and had to be left behind, as they were simply too big for her to carry. It was almost as if buildings had been constructed around some of them, allowing them to study the relics, though she understood why they were still trapped in their places. Most of those relics were incredibly old and had been impossible to interpret when she had used a singular essence. When she had used multiple essences, binding them together into unity, or at least a semblance of it, she started to have an easier time making sense of it. But she still didn't understand.

It felt as if there were answers just at the edge of her comprehension, and though she had been trying to dig into them, thinking that she might find something, she had so far not been able to learn anything more. The librarian had stayed, at least a manifestation of him had stayed, in some of the places with larger, more complicated relics. He left a part of himself open to Serena, active in her mind so that she might be able to tell just what he was doing, though she wasn't sure if there was anything in what he was doing that mattered until he had an understanding. That was what they were after, after all. She needed to know and be able to see what he was doing and what they might be able to find from it.

Tessatha came with her. She was quiet, though it seemed as if she were often quiet, something that Serena wasn't sure if it was tied to the unknown about what they were dealing with, or perhaps something that Tessatha still struggled with given everything she had gone through to get to this point. Either way, she wasn't going to interrupt. Sometimes when Tessatha was quiet, Serena had noticed that she would speak after a while, remarking upon some observation she had made. She had a good mind and was one of the best scholarly companions that Serena had ever had.

Strange that it should take us being separated by such time for me to find somebody like her.

If Tessatha had not been trapped as she had been, Serena may never have known her. And she may never have known what it was like to have a companion like her, somebody who could study and analyze and try to find answers the way Serena wanted. She couldn't help but feel as if she were lucky to have encountered her.

"Are you sure it makes sense for us to bring this back to the palace?" Tessatha asked, finally speaking as they neared the outskirts of Serena's homeland.

Serena had not been going too quickly, as she had been trying to drag the relics with her, feeling like she needed to have an opportunity to study them. Not only her, though. She wanted to give Raolin a chance to study them, as she suspected he would learn more.

"I'm not sure whether it matters what we bring them anymore. I don't know if any of these are active, at least until we place power into them."

Tessatha looked down at the bundle that she had. Some of them were made of metal, some stone, and a few were linked with essence as they had obviously been made of wood that had crumbled over time. It made it more difficult for them to really understand what might be within some of those different relics, but they were both determined to try to understand it. Each of them had a connection to the different types of essences, but then there was something else with it, as well, something that suggested that there was a power that was tied to unity. Even more than that, though, was the power that was within the relics they had uncovered so far seemed to be more potent than what they had uncovered before. It was almost as if each relic they found had more power than the last.

Either that, or with the rising intensity of the unity around them, power had started to change in the realm, and had become something more. She wasn't sure what to make of that, either.

"It all makes a difference," Tessatha said. "But perhaps the location of the artifact is the key. We might understand their purpose if we can find where they need to be."

She looked over to Tessatha, who was floating next to her. They didn't travel quickly, but flying this way was generally fast anyway. She hadn't even considered the possibility that the relics might have a particular place they needed to be. Maybe that was a mistake.

"Do you think that you and Arowend had moved them?"

Tessatha's brow furrowed for a long moment, and then she shook her head. "I don't remember. I don't think so, though. Arowend was quite particular about such things. He never wanted to move anything until we understood if it was bound to a specific location. That is why some of those buildings were like you saw."

Serena had thought that it was only because of the size of the relic, not because they wanted to preserve the relic where it had been uncovered, but that made a certain sort of sense, too.

"I think if we can understand the writing, we might be able to know more about where they belong. Or if we can figure out a way to activate them, there might be something within the relic that will help us determine more."

Tessatha nodded, but Serena could tell that she wasn't quite convinced.

And for her part, Serena wasn't quite as convinced, either. Would it make a difference? She remembered where they had uncovered these relics, and thought that she could return, if necessary, but at the same time, she wanted to have a place where they could sit and study, but it was even more than that. She was curious about the unity, whether there was anything within the relics, and the connection they shared to the unity, which might help them understand more about the power flowing through this land. Serena felt like that was going to be the key to everything.

"Look at the palace," she said, changing the topic.

They were nearing the outskirts of the city. From above, Serena was aware of the different types of power that flowed throughout the city, which seemed to fill each sect, though it was all tied to fire. Given the bound energies she now possessed and the way that the unity essence seemed to be shifting through her land, she recognized that the connection to these others also began to change. It didn't seem to be any weaker, as that was the concern that she and Maggie had shared, but it was certainly altered in some manner. She still didn't know how things would change for those who were of lower progression.

Many of them, including dragon forged, dragon skin, and dragon touched, relied upon the essence they had consumed, so she doubted there would be much difference for them. It was only once they reached dragon hearts that things really began to change, but even then, it was difficult to gauge, as the power within them was still tied to the essence they possessed. At least, that was the way it had been for Serena. She wasn't sure if it would be the same for others who were continuing to progress, especially at this time when things were changing. By the time a person reached dragon mind, and they were aware of the essence around them much better than they would've been otherwise, they should feel something more, but even then, it would be incomplete. It would be nothing like what it was as a dragon soul—and there were not enough dragon souls in this realm.

"I see what you're talking about," Tessatha said.

She had moved forward and now hovered above the palace, though not lowering down toward it. Serena had been distracted by the city itself, and the people within it, though she hurriedly caught up to Tessatha, wanting to be able to work with her as they studied the palace. Serena thought that she needed to focus on the palace and what they could uncover from it. An essence had changed within it and continued to change, but they weren't entirely sure what that meant.

"It started to shift when I began to activate some of the old places," Serena said. "I wasn't sure if it was significant, but I felt the unity starting to slide into the palace."

"And the palace is one of the oldest places in your realm," Tessatha said. "Bound to fire, or it had been, in ways that others had not been."

She wasn't seeking confirmation, and she was merely remarking, Serena realized. She watched as Tessatha circled above the palace, focusing on her essence, and letting it probe down from her, sweeping toward the palace itself until it touched the uppermost aspects of it. There was a bouncing of power, something that Serena could feel coming from it, but she wasn't quite sure what more to make of it, only that the strange bouncing of energy that had begun to build seemed to be tied to the unity that Tessatha was drawing upon.

Serena modeled the same essence and drew upon it to help Tessatha, but she realized it wouldn't make any difference. She had already felt the unity within the palace. Even if she hadn't felt it, she didn't need to probe in the same manner, as she could feel it much more easily. It was a natural connection, something that she could detect because of her connection to the palace.

"Do you think the other places like this have changed?"

Serena frowned. "I... Well, I haven't thought about it that much. But you're right. They probably have."

Tessatha looked at the bundle of relics in her arms. "What do we do with these?"

Serena had thought that they were going to be able to keep them safe and study them, but if she went with Tessatha, the way that she suspected that the other woman intended, then they wouldn't have any way of protecting the relics. Until they understood them and had an opportunity to know better what kind of power they possessed, she wasn't going to leave them behind, especially not if her mother was here and trying to harm them.

And so, she debated. "I think we keep them with us."

"Fun," Tessatha said with a hint of a smile. "Where first?"

"The Borderlands."

She moved quickly now, focusing on the power within her, and burst toward where Rob had described the testing location in Maggie's realm. Even as she traveled, she didn't need to worry about how she was going to find it. She could feel it.

There was something about that power that was drawing her, and guiding her forward. The unity was flowing through here, as well. The garden that sat atop where Rob had performed his testing and where Rob had connected to Serena and the others so that they could receive their testing, had not really changed. The colors of the flowers were the same, and there was a vibrant energy that radiated from it, along with the lovely fragrance that came, but now there was something more. And that something more seemed to be tied to unity. Serena felt the unity flowing everywhere. It was concentrating here, though. It was changing here. She hadn't done anything to this place to make it change, though.

"The same," she said to Tessatha as she caught up to her, and they both looked down upon the flowers. "I imagine it's going to be the same everywhere."

"Do we check?"

"I have a better idea," she said.

She closed her eyes and focused on her dragon mind linked to the other dragon's blood. Gregor was there immediately, as she felt his stony presence, and she dragged him toward a manifestation, where they floated in the air. She sensed Gregor's reluctance, as he never cared for the separation from his realm, even though he had become a true dragon blood, bonded to each of the essences. She described what had happened, and Gregor frowned, flickering for a moment, before he reasserted himself within the manifestation, more solidly this time. Now he seemed to be fully there, and as he looked at her, his manifested eyes showed a bit of concern.

"It is changing," he said, again.

"That's what I suspected," Serena said, as Tessatha joined them, drawn into this manifestation in the air by Serena's effort. "We see the same in other places. I suspect it's going to be the same in Rob's realm, and probably the same in the storm cloud."

"What does this mean for the rest of us?" Gregor asked.

"For us," Serena said, and she looked around, waving her hands briefly as she turned her attention back to Gregor, "I'm not so sure that it means much of anything. We have access to our essence, and given that we are somehow tied to the unity, we should be able to continue to access it even though we don't have Rob's connection to it. It's what happens later that has me questioning."

"I will look into this for my kind," he said.

"Thank you," Serena said.

With that, Gregor vanished.

She focused on the storm cloud, and though she hadn't spoken to him in quite some time, she felt his presence in her mind. He resisted her attempt to pull him into the manifestation, so she used the dragon mind connection to speak to him. Across the distance, his voice echoed through her, crackling with a sort of energy that she attributed to him. He was silent for a long moment when she shared the change in the different powerful locations. She thought that something had happened to the connection, but then his voice returned, and she was hesitant.

"It has changed," he answered.

"All of the places, then," she said.

"So, it seems. This unity. What does it mean for us?"

"I don't know. I think it means that we need to progress as Rob did," Serena said. "And I'm not entirely sure how we need to do it, though perhaps we need to go into the nexus as well."

"I have tried," the storm cloud said.

It was a surprise, though perhaps it shouldn't be. Why would it make a difference if others attempted to enter the nexus? It was what Serena thought that she would have to do, and she knew that others were going to need to do the same thing, primarily so that they could continue to gain the kind of power that they would need to have to withstand the heralds, and then whatever was coming after it.

"What happened?" Serena asked.

"Nothing."

"Then maybe there's something more to that progression than what Rob revealed," Serena said.

"We must speak to him."

"I will," Serena said.

The storm cloud disappeared, and Serena turned her attention back to Tessatha, stepping out of manifestation. Once she did, she found Tessatha watching, and there was something unreadable in her eyes.

"What do you think we need to do now?"

"The unity tower," Tessatha said. "If these other places are changing, it begs the question as to what is happening there. That is the first strangeness we uncovered. Somehow, all of this is likely tied to that."

She nodded, and she followed Tessatha, heading toward the unity tower. As they approached, Serena realized that it had changed. It was twice the height that it had been before. It seemed to be more solid, and thicker along the base, as well. It practically gleamed against the sunlight, as if it were glowing. There was quite a bit of power within it. More than Serena could ever have imagined.

But it was more than just that power. She felt a connection that had been forged. It seemed to be connected to the land, not to the land. It was almost as if it were connected to something deeper, something...

To the testing places, I've just visited.

That was what had happened. The palace. The garden in Maggie's realm. Someplace in Rob's realm. To Gregor. To the storm cloud. Even to water and thorns. All of it was linked to this.

It all seemed to be radiating power through the tower.

But it wasn't just flowing in one direction. It seemed like the power was going from the tower to those other places and back. It was pulsating, reminding her almost of a pulsing and beating heart.

She looked over to Tessatha, who was quiet.

"I think we need Rob's help here," she said.

"What do you think Rob's going to be able to do about this?" Tessatha asked, softly. "This is amazing. This is unlike anything I've ever seen before, at least I can remember. It is power. Real, raw power."

She could feel it.

And it seemed to be pressing something through her as if it were doing something to her. She felt drawn to the tower, though she wasn't sure if that was the right thing for her to do.

There was a danger to that kind of power, she knew. Even though she couldn't tell what it was, and whether there was anything within the tower that she had to be afraid of, she felt that danger deep in her core, as if it were trying to cry out, warning her about what was there, and whether there was anything more that she needed to be careful about.

She opened her conduit, trying to reach for Rob.

She could feel him, but she also sensed…

Distraction.

Whatever was happening, Rob was busy.

And she hated to bother him when he was busy, but she hurriedly sent through the connection, warning him of what was happening here, letting him know that some part of the unity tower was shifting.

"I started to wonder if all of this is tied to pure essence," Serena said. "The unity seems to strike me as something like that. When I was younger, everybody wanted pure essence. It was useful to all. And now…"

"If this is pure essence, then anybody could take it, and they could be… Well, anything," Tessatha suggested.

Serena nodded. That was her thought, as well.

And if they could be anything, what did that mean for them? What did that mean for the realm?

It felt as if this was something beyond her, at least in her current state. If she had progressed, she might be able to understand better the unity and the way that power flowed, but…

"Serena?" Tessatha asked.

Serena looked over and realized that Tessatha was now behind her.

She had been drawn forward. Not by her own intention, but because the unity tower itself was pulling on her, in some regard.

"What are you doing?" Tessatha asked.

"I can feel something," Serena said. "I can feel..." She wasn't even sure what she was feeling, only that it was drawing on her, dragging her forward, and...

And she didn't have any control over it.

Now it seemed as if the tower itself were pulling her forward, dragging her toward it, and dragging her toward that pulsating power that seemed to be echoing in time with some part of Serena. Tessatha grabbed for her, but she was not quick enough. Serena was drawn to the tower, Tessatha clutching her hand so that they were pulled forward.

By the time they reached it, a door had opened about midpoint along the tower, and it swallowed them both.

Chapter Thirteen

ROB

Rob braced himself. He wasn't even sure that he be able to handle a single subherald in his current state, but at this point, he wasn't going to stand down from a fight. He also thought that he needed to do anything he could for him to get free, as he had heard Serena's call for help. It *had* been a call for help. She had recognized some danger, and even though she hadn't alerted him completely about that danger, Rob knew that something had happened in his realm that they needed him for.

And if he wasn't there...

What was going to happen if he didn't reach them? He was the dragon unity essence bearer, and he was the one that they could rely upon for help, but if he was stranded, Rob knew what was going to happen. He would fall. The Eternal might escape.

And then...

And then the heralds would come, and whatever else

was out there would come, and his people would suffer and fall.

Rob refused to allow that.

He drew the unity realm into himself.

It collapsed the realm entirely, but he didn't need that tethering him. He needed the power, instead. And he targeted the nearest of the subheralds and focused on the essence he felt around him.

They were trying to use their essence to link in a way that would block him inside. Rob had felt something similar before, and he recognized that technique. If he could disrupt it, he might be able to break free, and then withdraw quickly enough to reach his realm, where he needed the power.

Run.

That was the thought that stuck with him.

And still, Rob hated the idea that he was talking about running, but as these subheralds swirled around him, he couldn't help but feel as if what he needed was to run to regain the power that he wanted. They were inhuman, and though they had humanlike arms and legs, that was the only part of them that struck him as human. Their birdlike heads and massive beaks left him filled with disgust. And the wings that battered at the wind, swirling around him, seemed to be filled with a measure of essence that was linking together, using that to try to target him.

He thought about how he was going to escape and realized that the technique depended on how he targeted them. He blasted essence, and as soon as he did, he began to feel some of the pressure on him beginning to ease. Whatever they were doing started to fade, giving Rob a chance to blast through them.

Just a chance.

He shot forward.

Two of the subheralds closed in on him.

Rob spun, shoving a burst of unity out from his palm, striking one of the subheralds in the chest, before spinning back and turning to the other that closed in on him. This subherald wrapped its wings around him just as Rob shot another bolt of unity at it. The unity bounced toward Rob, who drew that essence back into himself, bracing for another attack.

At least it seemed as if one of the subherald had fallen, dropping to the water below, leaving Rob with four of them.

Four now. How long before more come?

He doubted they had much time at all.

Those four circled him, and it seemed to Rob that they only really needed four of them to collapse essence upon him so that he could no longer attack quite as easily. Still, they gave him more space than they had before. Rob focused on the unity inside of himself. He felt a limit to what he possessed that he had not felt before. He was tempted to draw on Serena, and as he opened himself to the conduit, he found that his awareness of her was simply gone.

That was odd. There had never been a time when the conduit had failed him like this, but now that he needed it and that connection to Serena, there was no sense of her.

What of the other dragon blood?

He strained, quickly reaching out to them, trying to connect to them as much as he could so that he could try to feel for something more, and thankfully he began to feel some power building around him, through him.

Arowend pushed.

"I will come," Arowend said.

"No. It's not safe."

"We cannot lose you," he said.

"No," Rob said.

And then he turned. Four subheralds, he could handle that.

Take out one at a time.

But even as he started to focus, the subheralds began to shriek. Their massive beaks began to rip at the air in front of him as if they were trying to shred his essence, which was *exactly* what they were doing.

He could feel the essence starting to strip away from him, and he recognized the way that they were pulling on that essence, tearing parts of his unity away. He was bound to that power but wasn't as strong as he would be in his own realm. And they seemed to recognize that. More than that, they were working together, using a layer of power that stripped at him, and began to shred through everything he could do.

He pushed outward, but that was a mistake.

The subherald began to rip at that essence again the moment that he did, shredding it. It took Rob's focus to pull its essence back into himself, and to bridge it back into unity, and he knew that he was going to have to be much more careful here.

The subheralds were trapping him.

He thought about going down into the water, as it did seem to him that there was a limit to how far they would be able to go, but the moment that he focused on the water, he began to recognize that there was another essence down there that was a swirling deep beneath the surface, a threat to him.

So, he did not move.

He was going to have to try to find an opportunity to attack in the middle, but he didn't see an opening, though. The subheralds were circling, and there was a pattern to the way that they were moving, as if there was a link to how they were using that power. He could imagine some blending of energy, but until he had a way of finding it, he wasn't sure how it would work for him.

Could he disrupt the *pattern?*

He thought doing so would involve pushing through essence, but it might involve the kind of essence that Rob wasn't sure he could summon enough strength with.

He tried something different. He braced himself and focused on the nearest subherald he had drifted toward, targeting its eyes.

A burst of energy came from beyond him.

At first, Rob thought that there were more subheralds coming his way, but the burst of energy was familiar to him. Not subherald energy. Not the shrieking of these horrifying creatures. It was something else.

He focused, holding onto the power within himself, trying to brace himself for that essence and what was coming but was also ready for the possibility that there was something else he might need to deal with.

He saw faint clouds coming toward him.

Storm clouds?

No. It wouldn't be the storm clouds. They were too far away.

Alyssa.

But they had run.

A blast of essence struck one of the subherald, and it turned.

The shifting caught that subherald off guard, and the others were caught by it. Their pattern changed. Rob was aware of it the moment it did, and he reacted, sending out a blade of unity, striking the nearest subherald in the eyes the way he intended. The subherald dropped.

Now there were three.

Or two, Rob realized. The subherald that had turned had been battered by attacks, a series of blasts that came from Alyssa and the others with them. It shredded the subheralds wings and then began to target its torso, while Rob sent another blade of unity into the back of its head.

Two subheralds remained.

And then they shrieked before streaking quickly away.

He breathed a sigh of relief.

He called upon the essence that he had within himself, and then even drew upon the essence down in the water, calling it up into himself, devouring it with some aspect of the unity that shifted it. He hadn't attempted that before, which was probably a mistake. He had that ability and might need to use it here.

Alyssa rejoined him. "You were too slow."

"Thank you. I was trying to run, but they surrounded me."

"How many?" Alyssa asked.

"There were five."

She nodded. "And you survived. Congratulations. You have officially done something that we have not. The most that we have survived was three."

"Well, I think we killed three," Rob said. "Two got away."

"Which means that we won't have time."

"I think that we need to take the time that we have," Rob said. "There must be something here. There is an essence, much like I suggested, and we need to use that so that we can understand that there is something, but—"

"They came here with the subheralds, which means that once they escaped, they are going to go back to the heralds, and they are going to warn them. Once a herald comes, we won't be able to withstand it. *You* won't be able to withstand it. I know you're powerful and managed to capture the Eternal, but even you have limits, especially out here, separated from your realm and your power."

Rob continued to draw upon the essence beneath him, calling it into himself and processing it in a way that allowed him to turn it into an aspect of unity. It was slow work, but it did give him access to more essence than he would've had otherwise. But would it be enough to help him in battle?

It might not be enough. And he might not be able to do it fast enough.

"We have time. Give me this time. There is the essence here. You wanted answers, didn't you? You want to progress, don't you? This is where we find out if there is a possibility for that. Come with me, see what there is and if we can do this."

She breathed out heavily, and she looked at the others with her. "I don't want anything to happen to them."

"Then send them away."

"That's not how we do things," Alyssa said.

"Then give me the time," Rob said.

He wasn't sure what she was going to decide, or whether she was even willing to do this, but at the same time, Rob thought that the key to his understanding, was testing for something that would be akin to unity. He believed that there had to be something like it. Alyssa and the others with her had too much power, and were too similar to him with their power, for there not to be something like that. It had to be the key, didn't it? And if they could find that and a way to help her progress, he had to believe that they might be able to withstand the next attack.

What about the one after that?

Rob tried not to think about that, trying not to think about what everything was going to entail, and what he was going to involve him doing, knowing only that he had to take one step at a time.

Alyssa watched him for a moment, and then she nodded.

He turned, focusing on the land that was near him. This was the first place where he had felt considerable essence, and it was a place he suspected was tied to Alyssa, even though he didn't know that with any certainty. He felt something, a reflection of energy, that seemed to be tied to her. Maybe they could use that if he could better understand it and help her better understand.

If nothing else, she might be able to draw some of that essence into her so she could hold it into her portable realm again.

She stayed by him. "There is the essence here," Rob said again, trying to keep his heart from beating as wildly as it wanted. Given everything that they were dealing with, and the fact that the subherald had come at them, he knew that they needed to be quick, but he also knew that he wasn't going to be able to find the answers if he went quickly. "Can you feel it?"

"I can feel it," she finally said, with a pained expression.

"Good. What we're looking for is something different. Deeper. It's a connection of different types of the essence. I don't have your type of essence, though I don't feel like our essence is all that dissimilar," he said, focusing on her as he had before, and realizing that she did have connections to fire, earth, ice, and water, much the same way that he did. "You're going to need to help me with this."

"I spent many years here," Alyssa said softly. "And there is nothing here. You can search all you want, but I have scoured this land, and there is nothing. No way for me to find anything to progress."

Rob believed there had to be something here, even if she did not. His problem, though, was that even if there was some way of progressing, would it be potent enough? The unity had a significant store of power that he had used, drawing that outward through him, and then pushing it out into his land. It might already have been dispersed if they had something like that here. Or it might've been drained, given that she had spoken of the heralds acting like parasites, consuming all the essence. That fit with what he suspected happened.

But essence returned.

Not powerfully, certainly, but there was some form of it.

Alyssa hovered above one aspect of the island. This land was flat, smooth, and barren. Rob was left wondering what it would've looked like at one point, back when essence would've flowed through here, back when it would have been teeming with life, people, and cities. How many essence memories remained here?

Probably none, he realized. If the essence had been drained, essence memories would've also been stripped away.

And that was another complication of the heralds and whoever they served trying to target his land. There were still so many essence memories there that had not been lost to time that Rob needed to dig into to understand what had come before them. Memories that he knew Serena wanted.

Once again, he tried to open himself to the conduit, testing whether Serena was there, but there was an emptiness as before. The conduit simply went into nothingness.

How is such a thing even possible? Where had Serena gone?

He tried not to think about what that meant, not

wanting to worry about her, but he couldn't shake the underlying worry that lingered. He did send a message to Arowend, letting him know that something had happened to Serena, and asking him to investigate. Arowend responded and told him that he would.

"My home was down here," Alyssa said. "It was a long time ago, but I can still feel it."

Rob looked over. "You can feel it like you can feel an essence memory?"

"I can feel it like I should be connected to this," she said. "I kept the memories," she said, waving her hand toward the clouds surrounding her.

Rob hadn't realized that was even possible. But then, if she had gathered essence from her realm, she would've probably gathered essence memories in the process, linking all of that together. And that would have allowed her to hold onto parts of her land that would've otherwise been lost.

Maybe there were aspects within the essence memories that she had gathered that they could use. He didn't know if there was anything there, but if so, they might need to dig into it so that they could find a way to understand it better.

"Do those memories tell you anything about what it was like before?"

"The memories tell me *everything* about what it was like before," she said softly. "That is what I rely upon. That is what keeps me going."

"We might need them. There must be some way to link to it, but I'm not sure what it is."

"Neither am I," she said softly.

Rob let her move, and he continued to search, looking down at her land. There was essence here, much like he had believed, but the essence he detected did not give him any sort of the same sense he had with the unity. And without that, he was left wondering if perhaps there wasn't going to be any way for them to progress. Maybe that was what the heralds and whoever they served had been after. They had wanted to prevent progression.

And maybe that was why his land had now been targeted. They had begun to progress and begin to gain power. And they wanted to chase what the others did not want their people to find. If that were the case, then maybe Rob couldn't do anything different other than to continue to follow the unity, help his people, and perhaps bring Alyssa to his realm.

But if she came to his realm, there was no power there, not for her. Her essence was too different, he had seen. He could feel how different that was, as he could feel that there was very little, she could do to link to the kind of essence that existed in his realm. She was bound up to her own, and tightly enough that it should matter.

He drifted upward, and as he did, he found himself high above the ground, the water, and the others. It gave him a different vantage. He didn't have the tereagal eyesight, though if he did, he wasn't sure if he would see anything nearly as clearly as he would've liked. He wondered what might be out there, if anything. Maybe there was nothing for him to see but the vast emptiness that existed down below. Or perhaps…

He saw the different lands, everything that had

spread beneath him, and the way it existed, drawing outward. From up here, Rob could even see and feel some of that essence in a way he had not been aware of before.

And for the first time, he thought that he understood.

He had been trying to follow the distinct, separate realms, but now that he was here, he realized that was a mistake. There were no distinct realms down below. These were all a part of a singular type of realm. These islands were all linked, much like his realm had all been linked.

Or they should have been.

They no longer were.

He stared, watching the essence. He didn't recognize the different types of it, but he could feel something.

He focused on the unity within him. As he did, he began to feel a faint reverberation, a pulsation, as if there was some part of that essence that wanted to share with him an answer of what it could be. Rob didn't know what it was, only that he could feel it and the way it was down there, straining as if to try to provide him with some answer that he should be aware of. And as he focused, he started to recognize the source of it.

It was deep.

And it was nearby. Not on Alyssa's island, but somewhere close. Close enough that Rob thought he could help.

He started down toward her, wanting to share what he'd uncovered, when he recognized something else. Power was pressing toward them. It was coming quickly.

Subherald power.

Perhaps more.

And if the heralds were coming, did they have time to help Alyssa and the others progress? Rob wondered if perhaps the better question was could they afford not to take the time to let them progress, if such a thing were possible.

As he neared her, he knew what he was going to have to do.

He had to buy them time.

He had to help them find unity. He had to make sure that they could know what could be, and he had to ensure that he helped them so that he had allies against this coming threat.

Chapter Fourteen

SERENA

THE SUDDEN SURGE OF POWER THAT PULLED SERENA WAS overwhelming. She recognized the sense of it, as she had a familiarity with the unity to understand just what had pulled her, but it was an enormous draw of energy and seemed as if it were suddenly drawing on her in a way that she could scarcely fathom.

She felt the unity as it swirled, pulling upon her, dragging her—and Tessatha—away from where they had been and toward the tower. She feared that she was going to slam directly into it, given the speed with which the tower was pulling upon her, and the force of the essence that was working against her, but as they neared, some strange and enormous opening began to form at the side of the tower.

There wasn't anything inside of her essence reacting to the tower. It was reacting to something else. It was reacting to the essence around her. To the unity.

Or perhaps, she realized, it was reacting in some way

to Tessatha. If that were the case, they needed to be cautious, as Serena didn't know whether something that she had done in the past, back when she and Arowend had been researching the different powers in the world, would have triggered something for the tower.

She floated inside, and then darkness.

Everything seemed to be filled with power, though. Serena was aware of it, and she could feel the energy that was there, pressing upon her, in a way that left her trembling with it and trying to make sense of just what was that she felt. It seemed to come from all around, and energy that radiated, pulsing, and…

Flowing.

She had been aware of that sense as she had felt essence all around her in the landscape as she had been testing different towers, temples, and places of power. She didn't know that she would find anything quite like this, but now she felt some part of it and recognized that there was something there that she might be able to pull on, if only she could recognize the power, she could draw from it.

Tessatha was next to her. Serena was aware of the other woman, but only through the dragon mind connection, not because she could see her. She saw nothing. Everything around her radiated a sense of unity, to the point where even Serena's understanding of other essences seemed to be fading.

"How is this possible?" Tessatha whispered, the question coming through the dragon mind link.

They were floating, and through that floating, Serena felt the energy holding her up, propping her above the ground, or perhaps it was just holding her. Cradling her. Maybe there was nothing she could do against it, and she would have to find some way to fight her way free.

"I don't know," Serena said. "I'm not entirely sure what happened here, only that I can feel…"

She wasn't even sure what she could feel. Power?

There was a certain element of power here, but she wasn't sure if it was only the power that she was detecting. Maybe there was something more to what she was feeling here than what she had known before. She wondered if all of this was unity or maybe there was something else here. The tower was the question, after all. The more she learned about the tower, the more she felt the power within it, and the more that Serena questioned how much of the tower was designed and how much of it seemed to appear because of essence simply.

She dropped suddenly.

She braced herself, unsure what she would find, and landed on a hard stone floor.

She pushed herself up, and focused on the essence she could feel. All of them were still within her. She wasn't severed from her connection to the essences, so in that regard, Serena thought it was for the best. She was a little worried that she couldn't draw upon any of the other essences and that, somehow, the unity essence within the tower was going to sever that connection from her and keep her from having that connection, but thankfully that did not happen. She could not use them, though. Any attempt to do so left her feeling as if there was power there, but nothing more than that. She had access to essence, but that access wasn't enough for what she wanted to do.

She focused on the conduit that she shared with Rob, wanting to share with him what had happened, but as soon as she tried to call upon that connection, she found it missing.

Not that the conduit was not there. Serena was aware of the conduit and thought that she might be able to find some way of connecting to him, but there was a missing sense of power she normally felt when she attempted to reach for him through the conduit. She was cut off from him, much like she was cut off from her essence.

And now they were trapped inside this tower.

"Can you reach for your essence?" Serena asked.

"I can feel it," she said. "But as soon as we came inside the tower, I wasn't able to do anything with that essence. I thought that maybe you might be able to do something, but it seems as if that is not the case."

Serena looked around. Everything was dark, but not entirely dark. The more she began to look around and try to survey everything inside of this tower, the more she started to question if there was something she could find here. The walls seemed to glow with a soft light. Essence, she suspected, even though she wasn't sure if she could tell anything from the essence within the walls. She could feel it, though. It was unity, and given that she could feel it all around her, she recognized that power had to be everywhere.

"So, we're inside the tower, and we have to figure out what reason the tower essence brought us here," she said.

"I think we should be more concerned than that," Tessatha said.

Serena looked over to her, and Tessatha was turning in place, moving slowly. Serena realized that she was able to see Tessatha doing, something that she hadn't been able to do before. The fact that she could see something suggested that the faint light around them was enough for her to do that. And she started to recognize that there was more of a glow around her than she had noticed before.

"What else do you think that we should be concerned about?"

"Think about the palace that you lived in," Tessatha said, finally coming around to look at Serena. "A place of power, right? But it's a place of almost *inordinate* power. To the point where you would almost have thought that it was progressed itself."

Serena frowned, and then she realized what she was getting at.

The palace and other places like it were incredibly powerful. She and Rob and the others who had gone into those places had begun to question if those places had their own kind of consciousness, some part of them that had progressed to the point where they were able to make choices, and influence in the way that somehow those entities thought they needed to.

The unity tower was something else entirely. It comprised the unity essence and seemed to be drawing upon the other essence of the realm, pushing and pulling from those other great places. That might mean it was sentient in its own way.

There would have to be careful.

"What do you propose we do?"

"I think we need to figure out what the tower wants from us," Tessatha said. "Obviously, the tower brought us here. Or the essence brought us here. I'm not sure anymore, but something brought us here," she said.

Now Serena could see her much more clearly. The faint glowing was enough that she could see the other woman standing next to her, even though she couldn't see anything else from Tessatha, nor could she tell whether Tessatha was trying to pull up on her own essence. Serena sighed, disappointed, as she had grown accustomed to having access to other peoples of the essence and understanding what they were trying to do with it. It provided her with an advantage when trying to make sense of what was happening around her. Without that, what would she be able to do?

"How do we understand what the tower wants? If the tower wants something, should it try to tell us what it wants?"

"I think that it started to," Tessatha said. "It brought us here, and it seems to me that the act of bringing us here, guiding us inside of the tower's walls, suggests it is showing us what it wants. Maybe we need to explore and see what else is here to try to make sense of why it wanted to bring us here."

The idea that they would explore some random tower, some mysterious place, all on their own, was fascinating if Serena were honest with herself.

This was the kind of thing that she would've done before she met Rob, she would've gladly come to the tower, and taken the opportunity to explore something ancient like this, to try to make sense of whether there was anything here that she might learn, and anything that might help her understand what the people who had preceded them had known about power. And in this tower, given the markings on the surface of it, at least on the outside, Serena knew that there was considerable power inside of it, and a conceivable connection that seemed to connect to something more—the unity.

"Which way should we go?"

"I think we have to see what the tower lets us," Tessatha said.

She moved away from Serena and stopped near one of the walls, tracing her fingers just above the surface of it. She wasn't touching, though, almost as if she were afraid of what would happen if she made contact with the stone. The walls didn't change, but the glow brightened subtly.

"I can feel something here," Tessatha said.

Serena joined her, and though she didn't hold her hand out, she focused on the essence she felt around her. The unity was everywhere. Serena began to wonder if that unity was going to be the key to whatever they were trying to find.

Maybe the tower was trying to show them its purpose of it, drawing them inside so they could understand the reason behind the tower's presence and recognize what more the tower might be able to do for them—if anything at all.

"Let's explore this level first," Serena said.

They made their way around this level. It was wide

and open. The walls glowed softly, but there was nothing more than that. She thought that maybe she would find some symbols, markings, or writing that would provide greater answers, but as they surveyed the tower inside, she didn't see anything more.

She reached a door. When she motioned to it, Tessatha joined her. The door was set into the wall, the curvature of the wall making it look as if it were one of the tower's outer walls, but this was the only other door they had found on this level. Serena found that to be quite intriguing. The door was made of metal. As she neared, the door's color started to shift, becoming a bit darker. The shadows and gradations of darkness along the door shifted and began to take on different symbols and shapes that Serena thought might represent some of the writing they had seen on the outside of the tower.

"I recognize this one," Tessatha said.

"What does it say?"

"It's not a matter of what it says," Tessatha said. "As we never really broke down the language quite that well. It's too bad that your librarian isn't here."

Serena closed her eyes, focused on the librarian's manifestation, and wondered if she could connect to him, but even as she attempted to do so, and there was an emptiness. She wasn't hopeful, given that she couldn't even reach for Rob and had a better connection to him than she did to the librarian.

Only...

Maybe that wasn't quite true. With the librarian, he was a manifestation of the same kind of essence that Serena could command. So perhaps if she could draw upon the essence around her and find a way of drawing that power through her, she might be able to summon him again.

"I don't know if he's going to be accessible to us," Serena said. "So, the door," she said, and she turned to it. "You recognize this symbol, but do you recognize any others?"

"I think we need to test them," Tessatha said.

"How do you propose we go about doing that?"

"I think… Well, I think we need to pour some of… I guess we can't do that, either." She scrubbed a hand through her hair, and then looked to Serena. "Everything I would suggest is tied to essence, and in this place, we don't have access to any essence, so nothing that we could do, or would even consider doing, will work. So, I guess I would take any suggestions you might have."

Serena turned and focused on the door, the markings that were there. She could feel the essence within it. And as she looked at it, she started to wonder if this was the means of exiting the tower. There was no other way out; this level was all singular, with no stairs, doors, or other markings on the walls. So maybe the tower was testing them. It had drawn them inside, and it wanted to see if they were going to be able to find a way out.

She thought about what the librarian had taught her and the lessons she had learned over the time she had been connected to him from the different languages that existed. He had seen quite a bit; she had learned it from him, keeping it together and storing it. There were plenty of essence memories within her.

Essence memories. Maybe something here was an essence memory.

But she didn't have access to her own essence. She could use the unity, but not the way that Rob could. It made her frustrated at her ignorance. She hated that.

"Why don't we see if there are any symbols, we might be able to trigger anyway."

"I worry that the pattern might be significant," Tessatha said.

"Why do you say that?"

"Well, because the patterns are key to many things, especially in the older artifacts. You saw that in the relics we were uncovering."

Serena had been testing many of the relics, trying to make sense of what she could determine from the markings along their surface, but had not had an opportunity to test them as much as she wanted fully. But the artifacts did seem to have some significance with what pattern was placed. She had made a mistake by not taking the time to study them.

And even if she had taken the time, Serena wasn't sure it would've shown her much of anything. The only thing that the relics might have shown was that there was a pattern that was necessary for her to trigger, something that she already came to learn. So now she had to see if there was any way to open the door, but if they triggered the pattern in the wrong way, what would happen to them?

"Maybe we start with what we recognize," Serena said.

"It's dangerous," Tessatha said.

Serena looked around. The inside of the tower glowed a little bit more brightly. With every passing moment, she could feel that glowing, almost as if it were starting to build. And now that she paid attention to it, she recognized that there was something almost painful to the pressure of the essence. She hadn't been focusing on it before, but now the unity was building in a way that Serena could feel it seeming to creep through her as if it were trying to press through her own essence and remove it. If they stayed here much longer, there was no telling what was going to happen to them.

It was almost as if the tower *wanted* them to move on. If the tower wasn't going to tell them what they needed to do, or whether they needed to go, how were they supposed to move anywhere?

"I don't know that we have much more time here, anyway," she said. "I think the towers were trying to clarify that we need to get moving."

Tessatha turned, and she frowned. When she turned back to Serena, her brow was furrowed with concern. "I think we must do so quickly. I can feel something building, and more than that, I can feel as if something is coming."

That hadn't been Serena's experience, as she hadn't felt anything coming, but if Tessatha felt it, than Serena thought that they needed to take it seriously, as there was a very real possibility that they were going to be in danger.

So, she turned the door and focused on the markings. She searched through her memories, trying to find anything familiar to her. Several of them looked somewhat familiar.

As the unity essence continued to build, Serena tried to ignore it but found it increasingly difficult for her to do.

So, she started to touch the markings on the door. They formed a soft glow, as they pulsed. By the time she reached the fourth familiar symbol to her, the door pulsations had begun to increase with intensity.

She tried to brace herself, prepared for whatever was coming, but was not prepared for the door suddenly glowing, and for her and Tessatha to be drawn inside.

Chapter Fifteen

SERENA

The glowing lasted for only a moment.

Serena was ready for anything, or at least thought that she was. She had experienced the darkness before, and the steady buildup of light, and had been aware of the emptiness that had been around them before, so she thought that maybe they would end up on the outside of the tower, given that the door was situated as it was on the wall. But they were inside another room.

This was smaller. The ceiling was lower. She had to crouch down, so she didn't hit her head. The walls made her feel almost claustrophobic with the pressure she felt all around her, yet they were still alone. There was no glowing here, though there did seem to be some faint light that allowed her to see everything around her. She still couldn't reach her essence, though Serena immediately attempted to do so this time, not waiting to test whether there would be anything that would be lost to her. She focused on that essence, straining to see if there was going to be anything that she may be able to uncover, but even as she did, she did not find anything more than there had been before.

"This is not any better," Tessatha said.

"I don't think so, either," Serena said with a little bit of a laugh. It was a nervous laugh, though, and she looked over to Tessatha, who was crouched down, sliding through the room.

The room had to be twenty paces long, by ten paces wide, but with the low ceiling, it seemed as if it were even smaller than that. There were more objects in this than there had been in the other room. That had been a vast, space that seemed to occupy the entirety of the tower's space, whereas this was sectioned off, so she could imagine that there were other rooms outside. She saw no doors, though there had to be some other way out, wouldn't there? The last time, the door had simply appeared, so she was hopeful that something similar would happen here, giving them both a way to escape. Somehow. Serena didn't know what that was going to involve, but she increasingly started to think that there had to be an answer here.

She modeled her crouch after Tessatha and slipped along the wall. She reached for a small trunk. It was made of wood, though weathered and cracking, and the trunk itself seemed to be warm. She started to open it when Tessatha grabbed her wrist and frowned at her.

"Anything old could be dangerous," Tessatha said. "When we were relic hunting, we were always careful about opening such items, as there were many such things that could simply explode on us. Partly because they were meant to be trapped so that others would not be able to open them and steal the contents, but oftentimes because the relic itself is unstable, and over time, such instability began to build in the box, or whatever they were inside of, and the power was contained inside, but once you released it…"

"I think we need to see what is here," Serena said, looking around the room for a moment before turning her attention back to Tessatha. "The tower has power, right? It seems that if there is anything dangerous here, the tower should be able to contain it."

"I hope so," Tessatha said, her voice soft.

Serena pushed open the trunk, holding her breath as she did.

Then there was nothing.

She peered over the side of the trunk and looked inside.

There were three black metallic balls inside. She started reaching for one when she began to feel an energy beginning to build from inside it. She couldn't tell what it was, only that it seemed to be a power radiating from inside the box, and building with some strange energy intensity. It didn't seem to be unity, though, as Serena thought. She would've recognized the unity and known what to do with that. In this case, it seemed almost as if the essence here was a buildup, a contrary essence, to the unity, in a way Serena could not quite place. She focused on trying to make sense of it, but could not tell anything more. She looked over to Tessatha, who was leaning forward and frowning.

"I don't recognize it, either," she said.

"But it's a unique kind of essence, isn't it?"

"Of some sort," Tessatha said. "The real challenge, though, is what kind of essence it is, and whether there is anything there that we might be able to find. I start to wonder if perhaps there is something there that we shouldn't be able to test, something that we don't want to test," she said.

"I know," Serena said. "And yet, I feel like the tower is trying to guide us someplace, isn't it?"

"Is it?" Tessatha asked. "We're the ones who triggered the markings on the door. I would suspect that the ancients who knew about the tower, and knew what the power inside of it, would've known about how to trigger the doorways that existed to allow them to travel from one realm to another."

Realm.

Serena thought that Tessatha's choice of words was interesting, especially given that she chose the word realm, the way Rob described the spaces between the different lands. Maybe that was what they were dealing with now, some new kind of realm, someplace that would build a kind of power that they might be able to summon, perhaps even understand different kinds of essences. Maybe that was the point of the tower. It was a way for them to come upon more power, and to understand better it, and the connection that existed so that they might be able to use them.

Rob had been looking for ways to progress, and in this case, Serena started to wonder if maybe this was the key to it.

"Let's leave it here for now," she said.

"For now?" Tessatha asked, arching a brow at her. "Do you intend to return here?"

"Well," she began, and she looked over to Tessatha, before filling her in on what she thought about the realms, what that meant, and how she questioned whether the essence was going to be bonded together in a way that they were all supposed to find a connection. "If we manage to get through this, and we can get a hold of Rob, who has a better understanding of the unity essence, I wonder if perhaps we might be able to find something here that will help us better understand everything that's here, and better understand how we can use that, so yes," she went on, and looked down at the trunk. "If all of this is tied to different essences, maybe we need to return."

Tessatha nodded slowly. "Maybe that's what it is. Maybe what we'll find here are different types of the essence. And..." She frowned and looked around the room. "When I focus on what I can feel, I can detect a different sort of energy here. Maybe the tower is trying to squeeze us, or perhaps squeeze the essence that is here, making sure that we have an opportunity to feel something about it."

Serena hadn't even focused on that before, but it made sense now that Tessatha said it. There was energy here, and she wondered if she could find something within it to help her understand the different types of essences.

She moved on, crawling along the floor until she reached another trunk, only this one was shaped quite a bit differently. The other one had been rectangular, and this one was almost cylindrical, with markings along the surface of it. It looked to be lacquered, and better maintained than the last one, so as she reached for it, feeling more comfortable doing so. When she touched it, there was an immediate tingling through her hand.

She jerked her hand back. It was painful.

That pain began to crawl through her as if some part of her skin was burning. It worked its way up her arm, into her shoulder, and across her chest. The pain started to crackle inside of her.

Serena cried out.

Tessatha ran over, but Serena warned her off with a shake of her head. She didn't want anything to happen to Tessatha, as she didn't know what she had done, and by touching that item, she worried that she had somehow activated something, allowing some strange essence to creep through her. If that were the case, then Serena had to be careful. She didn't have any access to her own essence, so she couldn't use that to save herself.

But the essence was there, wasn't it? There shouldn't be anything within her that could be damaged, not with her own essence, and not with the other essences that she already bonded to. Those connected essences should be able to protect her and keep her safe so that she doesn't have to worry about anything more. She focused on that essence, ignoring the pain, though it was difficult for her to do so. That pain continued to crackle through her, and Serena worried about it changing her. She didn't know what she had touched, and she didn't know what it was going to do to her.

The essence within her began to radiate, and then…

She tried to bundle them together and turn them into unity, but there was no response.

She continued a bundled power-up, trying to tighten it down in a way that would protect her. The essence she felt outward was still crackling through her, but it seemed as if it were slowing. Thankfully.

Serena ignored the pain and continued focusing on her own essence. She had to find a way of piecing it together. She might not be able to control it outwardly, but she could use it inwardly. And at that point, that was all that she wanted.

Tessatha was watching her. Serena felt tears streaming down her eyes, or maybe it was just wet. Whatever it was, Serena felt overwhelmed. And she continued to try, she continued to work on the essence, and she continued to try building it inside of her.

And then there was a burst.

It was faint at first, but the fire started. Serena was so thankful for the moment that she felt that fire and knew that there was some part of her that was protected by that fire, the way that it was trying to build within her, trying to rise inside of her, and offer her a measure of protection she wouldn't have otherwise. She embraced the fire and then added each of the other elements to it, working from fire to ice, life, earth, water, storm, and bramble. Each of them mingled within her, adding additional layers of protection to her. One after another, they began to build. One after another, they started to rise inside of her, and one after another, they pushed outward, resisting whatever it was that had started to overwhelm her.

When it was done, Serena leaned back and sighed softly.

"That was unpleasant," she whispered.

"How did you stop it?"

"I can still feel the essence inside myself," Serena said. "And I can control that. I wasn't sure if it was going to work."

"We should both ensure, we can master that first," Tessatha said. She leaned back on her heels and closed her eyes for a moment.

Serena began to feel the essence coming off the other woman as she did. That was a subtle, but welcome change. In the time that they had been in the other aspect of the tower, they had been able to feel anything else, other than the power of the unity, so for her to detect anything, even minimally from Tessatha, left her thinking that perhaps they would find an answer here, and maybe they would be able to overwhelm the dangers that they had encountered. She wasn't sure if that was going to work, but so far, it did seem as if she was having some success.

Finally, Tessatha opened her eyes, and she looked over at Serena. "It's challenging, and it's almost as if the technique is different for reaching essence. I had to focus on my primary essence."

"I did the same," Serena said. "Fire burned through me."

"But then the others came easily," Tessatha went on. "And what was stranger was the unity, it felt different than when I formed it before. I wasn't sure why, but it did feel as if there was something, and some part of it, that I was supposed to use."

Serena also focused on the essence inside of her, and as she did, she started to bind them together. The unity she could feel was different and distinct from what she had used before. In this case, the unity was blending, but an incomplete sort of blending. Each of the essences was distinct and discrete as she was trying to form that unity. And perhaps it wasn't unity at all. Maybe that was the point. She had distinct essences.

But thankfully, by having those distinct essences, she had a way of defending herself from whatever it was that had nearly overwhelmed her.

She looked over to Tessatha. "This is powerful," she said. "I don't know what it was, but it hurt."

"Then we need to be careful with it," Tessatha said. "Whatever it is, and whatever it's trying to do to you, we shouldn't just go around touching everything."

Serena started to smirk. "Well, we're inside an ancient tower, and there is quite a bit of unknown essence around us, so maybe that's probably what we should have done from the very beginning."

"I tried to tell you that," Tessatha said.

"I know," Serena said. "And I didn't listen."

She looked down at the item, and now that she had the essence within her, and had a better sense of it, even if she couldn't express it outward, she wondered if she might be able to open the item more easily. Or maybe it wasn't meant for her to open.

But the moment that she had felt it, the moment that she had felt that power within it, Serena had recognized that something was burning with it, building through it as if it were going to pour out of her.

"There are other items here," Tessatha said. "We have to be cautious and careful, as everything inside of here could be incredibly dangerous to us."

It was good advice and was the kind of thing that Serena would normally be the one to say, but thankfully she had Tessatha with her. And Tessatha, being a scholar, somebody who had been a relic hunter in her time before she had been trapped by essence, had a very different understanding of the relics, and the power within them, then Serena did.

They were trapped inside some, possibly a sentient tower, with strange powers, and had no real access to their own essence. And until they had a better understanding of what was here, and what they were going to do, she wasn't sure that she was going to be able to escape, and she wasn't sure they were going to find their way to freedom. She had to be careful, and they both had to find something here, some way, for them to understand what was here, and whether there was anything more for them.

"We need to find a door," Tessatha said.

"You don't want to explore all of this?"

"I would love to explore all of this, but I think the entire purpose is for us to understand what's inside of the tower. There had to be some reason for us to be brought here. But now, I think that we need to see if we can find our way through." She paused, looking back at Serena. "Maybe you'll want to return, and perhaps bring Rob and his unity essence, but until then, I think we need to move through here deliberately."

They started along the floor. There was nothing. Just occasional trunks, old, worn shelves, and a small table at the center of the room. Low enough that Serena could not even get her legs beneath it. It looked as if it were made for somebody that was quite a bit smaller than her, though the entire room looked as if it were for somebody quite a bit smaller than her.

They tested several of the different boxes, different openings, and alcoves, and at each one, she began to find that there were different essences, but nothing more that would help her understand the purpose of what they were doing here, and whether they were going to be able to find any way out. As they searched, she continued sweeping around but found no door. As far as Serena could tell, they were trapped.

She stopped in the middle of the room, looking around. Though she could feel the essence around her, she wasn't sure that there was going to be any way for them to get free.

And worse, now that she had stopped looking, she was focused on everything around her and began to feel that unity essence once again. It had been a vague, constant companion before, but this time, as she paused here, she began to feel some part of that essence starting to pulsate and rise, building with a steady intensity to the point where Serena knew that if they didn't find her way free, they would be overcome by that power.

And as Tessatha turned to her, looking over to Serena, Serena was aware that the other woman felt the same.

"We have to find a door," Tessatha said.

"And quickly."

Chapter Sixteen

AROWEND

Arowend focused on Rob. He could feel him, as he had been increasingly aware of Rob since he entered the nexus. There was something about how he had changed, some part of him that had bridged the different essences and reverberated with some understanding inside of Arowend. It was almost as if Arowend should have some connection to what had happened to Rob, but he wasn't sure what it was.

The other man had proven himself incredibly capable, far more so than Arowend remembered being when he was still alive and not an essence manifestation. Then again, there were still gaps in Arowend's memory, enough so that he wasn't even sure if what he remembered was accurate. He did not know enough, and though he tried to make sense of those memories, some gaps could not be filled. Even Tessatha had not been able to help him fill those gaps.

Rob had gone beyond.

That annoyed Arowend. He tried not to let it bother him, but it did. He didn't like being left behind and didn't like the idea that he was not useful, but for the sort of things that Rob was doing, the kind of power he was wielding, perhaps Arowend *was* useless. He certainly couldn't use power in the same way that Rob could. He didn't have his unity connection, so he had limits to how far he could go. He was confined to this realm, and while that was an extensive area, and far more than Arowend remembered having been able to traverse before, at least easily, it was still not as far as Rob could go.

And he still didn't have Rob's ability to wield power.

Maybe in time, he could.

Or maybe never would. He was nothing more than an essence manifestation now, wasn't he? He tried not to let that bother him, but increasingly, it did. He felt as if he were incomplete. He missed his physical form, even if he wasn't sure what that mattered any longer. Having reached the essence he did and access to more essence than he had in his previous life, he should be pleased with what he had become as Arowend progressed here.

And that was what he had been after all along, hadn't he? He had wanted to progress, and he had wanted to know that power, and he wanted to find a way for him to understand all of that so that he might be able to master aspects of it that he wouldn't have been able to before. But even as he had done that, he still felt as if there were gaps in what he could and should be.

Arowend pushed those thoughts away.

He tried not to follow Rob and tried not to follow what he was doing, but even that was difficult. He felt as if he were chasing someone and something that didn't want him around. And maybe that was what it was. Maybe Rob didn't want him.

Or maybe it was just that Rob was busy.

He drifted.

In times like these, he took on a more nebulous form, allowing himself to simply drift, and did not focus on maintaining physicality. There was something quite relaxing about it, as he could not help but feel as if having this emptiness, and this openness, allowed him to simply be. He felt as if he were connected to the world in a way that he couldn't be when he was a physical manifestation. That was something that Rob and the others could not appreciate. And perhaps they never would. Then again, if they continue progressing the way Rob thought they would, he eventually would take on what Rob believed was a dragon form.

Arowend thought that such a form wasn't likely.

At least, it made sense with what he had seen, and the kind of power they had experienced, to the point where he could not help but believe that such a thing would be possible in time, but it would take the right kind of progression.

And what would that mean?

Those were the questions that Arowend didn't have the answers to, but then again, Rob didn't have those answers, either. They were looking for progression, looking for what it would take for them to be able to battle this other entity, an entity that the heralds served, but even Rob wasn't sure what that would involve.

He reformed, drifted down to the small temple, and

landed inside. He didn't go down to visit the Eternal. Rob hadn't forbidden it, and Arowend wasn't sure he would've permitted Rob to have forbidden it, but he did not want to disabuse Rob's trust. He had already done that enough, and he felt as if he were trying to regain it every day and with everything that he did. He needed to make amends for what he had done and what he had been. It was difficult. Especially when he was around others that remembered what he had been like, regardless of what form Arowend took on. Many of them recognized his essence, and they recognized what he had been, even if they didn't say anything. The only reason that many of them didn't say anything was because of Rob, and because he claimed that they needed to be forgiving.

But I caused so much suffering.

That was the hard part for Arowend to get past. He had caused so much suffering, and though he didn't want to have to relive it, there was a part of him that felt as if he had to make amends for what he had been.

That was what Tessatha had suggested.

And Tessatha was always the wise one. She had a quick and scholarly mind and had been the one to recognize dangers. She had warned him when the others were unhappy with his desire to form a unity.

Arowend lost control over his form for just a moment.

That was a new memory.

At least, that was a memory he had not recalled before. He struggled, trying to hold onto his structure, thinking that maybe there might be something he could recall if he were to track those memories down, but even as he attempted to dig through those memories, they were fleeting and difficult. There were answers within him, but those answers still seemed elusive.

How was he gaining new memories, though? He was an essence memory, essentially, so everything should be accessible to him, or so he thought.

That was something that he and Tessatha had been working on, trying to make sense of what it meant for him to have taken on this form, trying to understand what it would look like for him as he gained additional power, but maybe there wasn't anything that they could find, nor would there be anything that they would be able to use.

Maybe in time, he would be able to find additional answers, and would be able to dig through them, but for now...

For now, Arowend needed to stay focused.

He tested for a moment and felt the protections that secured the Eternal in place. There was always the concern that the herald would find a way to escape, but so far, he had not. He was locked in the prison Rob had created. At least, it *seemed* as if he were locked into that place. Part of the reason that Arowend had remained here, or at least kept part of himself here, was because there was the underlying fear that all of this was a trap. Why not? It would be sensible to create a trap like this, especially as it would permit others access to Rob and his realm, while they made other preparations.

It was the kind of thing that the Netheral would have done.

Arowend hated thinking like that, but he had to

acknowledge that as a real possibility. If they were using that kind of power and had access to so much strength that they did not exist in their realm, why was it so impossible to believe that they would be able to use that to trap them in some manner?

It wasn't hard to believe.

And though Arowend might be the only one to believe that, he wasn't about to let them surprise him.

He felt for Rob again.

He had been doing that too often.

Rob was battling. He felt it. He wasn't sure what he was doing, only that there was activity, and that Rob was in the middle of something dangerous.

"Do you need help?"

"There is nothing," Rob said.

"I can feel that you're busy. I don't know what it is, but—"

"I'm fine," Rob said." Stay there."

That was not all he said, but that was the gist of it, to the point where Arowend felt a surge of annoyance again. He reached for Tessatha and found her missing.

That surprised him. Most of the time, when he reached for Tessatha, he could feel some part of her. Ever since his return, along with her return, he had been aware of her in ways he hadn't before. Now what he felt was emptiness. It was almost as if she had simply vanished.

That couldn't be the case. Tessatha couldn't have vanished. Not unless she had gone with Rob, and he didn't think that was the case, as knowing Rob as well as he did, he wouldn't have brought anybody with him that would be placed into sort of danger that would have brought them away from their realm.

So not there.

Where, though?

He focused again, straining with his awareness, using the essence that he had. Given his understanding of essence, the unity, and his experience with the nexus, Arowend did know that he was better connected than some to this world, somehow bonded in a way that he had not been before, and bonded to this land in a way that helped him connect to it and understand the powers that were here.

The only one who had the same connection was Rob. But then, even Rob wasn't in the same form as Arowend. It was his essence form that gave him the opportunity, and gave him the ability, to test for things that even Rob could not do. He didn't feel anything. He had been searching, focusing, straining, and trying to make sense of what was out there, but even as he did, he did not find anything more.

That troubled him. There should be something, shouldn't there?

What about Serena?

Rob would be displeased if he knew that he was going after Serena, but she and Tessatha had formed a unique connection; the two of them had been spending quite a bit of time together. That time suggested that the two of them would be together now. So, he probed, hoping that maybe there would be some answer to what she was doing, something that he might be able to find to explain where she had gone, but…

He didn't feel anything.

Serena was gone, as well.

That startled him. He wasn't worried. At least, he was not worried enough that he thought he needed to react, but he was concerned.

Aren't they the same thing?

He pushed those thoughts aside.

He started upward, quickly transitioning out of the building and floating. He remained in his nebulous form for a long moment, allowing the air to carry him, focusing on what he could feel of Tessatha and Serena, thinking that maybe he could feel something of their essence, some memory that had lingered to try to get an idea of where they had been. That was a difficult use of essence, but it was something that Arowend could do. He allowed himself to disperse simply, spread outward, into thin tendrils of essence that extended like a fog that layered over the entirety of the realm. He hadn't done that too often, as there was some danger of losing control over it, but he had been testing how much he could spread outward, thinking that if he could find a way to use that connection, he might be able to express himself more, and might be able to find more power.

As he did, he recognized a bit of memory.

It was unexpected. It was a surge of power.

And it was near the tower.

He pulled himself back.

For a moment, there was a bit of resistance to doing so, almost as if some part of the realm were trying to stretch him thinner and thinner, straining against him, but Arowend was strong, and he had existed in this form for longer than most, so he was able to pull against that strain and to draw himself back into a reflection of himself until he tightened it up and streaked toward that tower.

Then he landed.

The tower looked even larger than it had before. Arowend was aware of the power that emanated from it, pulsating, as if something to it was alive, and given what he knew about essence, it probably was alive. He moved carefully toward it. This was where Tessatha and Serena had been. He was certain of it. He had felt some power against him, though he wasn't sure what it was. He could still feel their memory, but there was something else that he could also detect. Some aspect of power seemed to have changed, as if…

As if the tower had reacted.

"I'd be careful getting too close," a voice said behind him.

Arowend spun, immediately drawing upon his essence, and preparing an attack, before tamping down that urge.

Raolin.

It was strange seeing him. They had served together for so long, Raolin serving as the ice king while Arowend was the Netheral. But surprisingly, Raolin had not seemed to be offended by Arowend's change, if he was even aware of it.

He's aware of it.

There was something in the way he looked at him that suggested that he was fully aware of who Arowend was, and what he was. And still, there was no sign of judgment in his eyes. No sign of anger, which left Arowend feeling…

It left him feeling as if he needed to do something to make amends to this man. He had changed him. He had abducted, stripped away his essence, forced ice upon him, and made him serve.

All because of Arowend's rage.

Not mine. The Netheral.

There were times when they felt as if they were different things. There were other times when Arowend could remember what it was like as the Netheral, could remember what it was like when he had been filled with that anger, and could remember what it was like when he had wanted nothing more than vengeance for what had happened to him. At that time, that was the only thing that he knew. He had wanted that vengeance and to destroy those who had destroyed him, as it was the only thing he'd been able to think about, in that essence, part of him, the part of him that had survived when everything else had been destroyed.

"What happened?" Arowend asked, deciding to focus on the task at hand, and knowing that he was going to eventually come back and talk to Raolin about what they had done. He had to make amends with him just like he had to make amends with everyone.

"I don't know. I was here, studying the tower, when Serena and your friend came to visit. A door opened, and the tower swallowed them."

Arowend frowned. "The tower *swallowed* them?"

Raolin shrugged. "I know how it sounds. But that's what happened. A door," he said, and he pointed up the tower, to a space that looked about midpoint along the tower itself, "opened there, and they were drawn inside. I could feel some of the essence that was pulling upon them and didn't have an opportunity to react quickly enough to stop it."

"So, they are inside the tower?"

"Seems that way."

"Why?"

The question wasn't so much for Raolin, as it was for Arowend trying to make sense of what was happening, but Raolin surprised him.

"As far as I can tell, this tower is more of a construct than something real," he said. "Some construct, though. It seems to be comprised entirely of the essence. And as the unity, as Rob likes to call it, continues to build, spreading throughout the realms, this construct grows stronger. I think he was trying to make sense of how this tower could simply appear, or whether it had always been here and hidden, but everything I've identified so far suggests to me that it just appeared. Like a construct of the essence."

The idea seemed impossible, but then again, so many things when it came to essence were impossible, weren't they? Arowend's mere existence was impossible.

"Are they safe?"

He looked over to Raolin, who had frowned, pinching his chin with an ink-stained hand. Arowend realized the other held a notebook tucked under one arm, and a satchel slipped over his shoulder. This was not the kind of man that he had worked with before. This was somebody else. Raolin had changed.

So, have I.

"I can't say," Raolin finally answered. "Inside the tower, a construct like that, it's possible they have been brought for a purpose."

"What purpose?"

"Whatever purpose unity has for this realm, I suspect."

Arowend focused on Rob and tried to forge a connection between them. If anybody could do anything about this, then it would be Rob. He had a connection to unity in a way that Arowend did not, and he could use that to find a way to break into the tower itself and go after Tessatha and Serena so that they could find an answer about what had happened here.

But…

Whatever Rob was doing was important.

Arowend couldn't tell exactly what it was, only that he could feel something from Rob, some aspect of him that was pushing against him as if to keep him out. And perhaps that was what it was. Rob did not want anybody to bother him with what he was doing.

Instead of bothering him, Arowend sent a message.

He kept it short. He kept it simple.

"Serena and Tessatha are inside the tower."

He wasn't sure how Rob would react to that, and there was no real obvious answer from Rob, nothing to suggest that he was bothered by that, but he suspected Rob would take action. For Serena, Rob would do anything. That was Arowend's experience.

Wouldn't I do the same for Tessatha?

And he had.

That was the cause of his anger during his destruction. He had raged about what happened to him, but if it had only been him, Arowend thought that he might have been able to tolerate that. But what had happened to Tessatha, to the woman he loved, truly drove him mad.

And he was thankful he'd been brought back.

He looked over to the tower.

Tessatha had help with that. She had given what he needed to bring him back to where he was now, to give him an opportunity to become what he was now. And now she was inside the tower. He could feel the unity essence, the pulsating of power, and something about it that didn't feel necessarily malicious, but it didn't feel benign, either. It was dangerous.

Worse, they were inside the tower.

"I'm going in," Arowend said.

"There's no door," Raolin said.

Arowend began to separate, losing his form, and drifting upward. "I'm not sure that I need a door."

Raolin grunted. "Perhaps not. Then be careful."

He looked down and saw Raolin looking up at him, frowning. And...

And it seemed as if there was some recognition of Arowend. Recognition that he was another. Recognition of what Arowend had done.

But there was no anger.

"I will bring them back," he said.

And with that, he took off, floating, drifting, feeling the pull of the essence up ahead, and letting it carry him. As he neared the tower, he wasn't sure what would happen, if anything. It didn't surprise him when the essence began to pull upon him, on his nebulous form, dragging him toward the tower. It didn't surprise him when that power suddenly pulled with a drawing of energy, something more than what he could withstand. And it didn't surprise him when he felt unity essence wash over him, compressing him, squeezing.

The only thing that surprised him was when he emerged inside the tower.

Arowend had been forced into a physical form… and could not change it.

How was he going to find them like this?

Chapter Seventeen

SERENA

They scrambled around the room. They'd been checking everything, moving anything that they thought was safe for them to move and trying to pull it away from the walls, searching for anything that would give them an idea of where to find a door. There was nothing. Not like the last place, where the door had simply been there, and all he had to do was figure out how they wanted to activate it. In this case, the room itself seemed to confine them, trapping them in a way that left him feeling as if they were going to be overwhelmed by the power that was there.

The unity was building, and starting to squeeze, to the point where Serena felt that power was pressing inward upon her in a way she had not detected before. She did not care for it. There was a time when she had wanted the unity, trying to understand that essence, hoping that she might be able to gain some power with it, the same way that Rob had, though, when he had gone into the nexus and pushed that nexus energy out away from him, there had been a difference for him.

In this case, there was nothing like that. She wasn't going to have the same opportunity as Rob, and she didn't think she would be able to use the unity, not without having some new nexus form.

And maybe that was the purpose of the tower. Maybe the tower was trying to help them create a new sort of nexus, but why hold them here like this if that were the case? Why continue to trap them in a way that they couldn't escape?

"What if we move the table?" Serena suggested.

She'd been staring at it for far too long, trying to make sense of whether there was going to be any way to get free, but the only thing that she could find that was out of place was the table itself.

Tessatha crawled over to it and looked at it. "I hadn't even looked much at the table. It was just here. But look, Serena."

Serena hurried over to her, as fast as she could, given the low ceiling and how difficult it was for them to navigate through this. When she'd reached her, she looked down and saw a series of markings, much like the other door had.

"Do you recognize any markings here?"

The markings were much like the last one, and none of them was all that strikingly familiar. Some of them looked like symbols Serena had seen before, but without much of a way for her to make sense of them. She wondered if the librarian would have known anything, but then again, he was still struggling to piece together all the different aspects he had learned. He was changing, as well. Maybe as he continued to take on the unity essence, the librarian would begin to have more memories, but even if he didn't, they needed time to explore, understand, and try to make sense of what was around them.

"I've seen this one before," Tessatha said. "And this one." She pointed to a pair of different marks, each strikingly different from the other.

"Let's try them," Serena said.

"I don't know that I want to," Tessatha said, and she looked over to Serena, her eyes drawn. "I'm... well, I'm afraid."

Serena smiled at her. "I understand. I'm also afraid, especially because we don't know what will happen here, but can you feel the unity? It's starting to build, so I don't think we can linger here much longer."

"I..."

Serena reached forward, and she motioned for Tessatha to join her. She nodded to Tessatha. "Show me. We'll do it together."

Tessatha took a deep breath, then looked down at the table and pointed to several different markings. One of them looked familiar to Serena, and it took Serena a moment to realize why. It was the marking she had seen on the cottage that Tessatha had brought her to, where she and Arowend had once researched.

The unity essence pressing behind her was building with powerful intensity. She pressed on those markings. And then the door began to glow.

Unlike the last time or even the time before, Serena was ready for it. As that power began to build, the unity stretching, drawing into the door, and sweeping away from the room itself, Serena braced for the sudden change, and the drawing sensation she knew she would feel.

Then they were inside another room.

This one had an enormous, domed ceiling. The room was narrow, probably only fifteen paces to either direction and cylindrical, as if they were in some tall tower peak. She braced for the oncoming essence, worried that there might be some aspect of the unity that would start to push upon her, but there was nothing. They were safe.

"That was different," she said, looking over to Tessatha.

"I can feel…"

Tessatha began to look around her, and essence began to build within her. "Yes. I can feel my essence. I can use it more effectively, now, as well."

Serena frowned. Could she?

She hadn't even tried using her essence as she had a transition between the different rooms, though that was a mistake. That was something she needed to be testing every time they transitioned, because there was a greater danger every time, they made that transition.

Fire came to her easily. She expressed it outward, glowing in a barrier that radiated out and around her. She worked on the ice next, and then quickly each of the other aspects of the essence. She tried to blend them into the unity, using the technique that Rob and Arowend had taught her, but the connection didn't work quite as it should. There was some aspect that wasn't quite right.

But still, she had managed to use essence. That gave her a wave of relief.

"We can use it," she said, smiling at Tessatha. "That's good."

"Is it?" she asked. She had moved over to the wall and was not using her essence, but she was tracing her hand above the wall's surface, almost as if she had found some power within it. She finally touched the wall, and the surface of it began to glow with a little bit more intensity. Unity, or perhaps it was just one of Tessatha's essences.

Serena wasn't sure which it was, and she didn't know whether the woman was doing anything like that, or maybe there was some other aspect she was drawing upon. She wanted to be ready for anything coming from Tessatha or the walls. Anything might be dangerous, but this room felt… safe. Also, having access to her essence made her feel far better than before.

"Why would you think that it's not?" Serena asked.

"Why do you think that we have access to our essence?" Tessatha looked over at her, and her eyes showed a worried expression. "In the other places, we had access to no essence, and then you could use your internal essence, but only when you needed to find a way to heal yourself. Why do you think the tower allows us to use our essence here?"

"I suppose I don't know. Are you thinking something will happen?"

Tessatha continued to trace her hand along the wall, and as she did, she moved slowly, creating a circuit inside the room. "I just don't know. It seems to me that we have been finding dangers. Or at least the last place we found was dangerous. In this room... The fact that we have access to our essence, and the fact that we can continue to use it, leaves me to wonder if perhaps there is some other reason that the tower wants us to have that. What if..."

A strange cry cut her off.

Serena looked up. The cry came from overhead.

Everything was dark in the upper aspect of the tower, but she *felt* something that she had not felt before.

It was an essence, but it was a kind of essence that she had not felt before. This was powerful and dangerous. She focused on what she could feel and started tracing that power, trying to make sense of it. There was nothing.

But it was coming at them.

She erected a barrier around herself. There was a time when she would only use fire, looping it outward, and exploding that power in a way that would offer her a measure of protection. And the fire was still an aspect of what she was doing, but it wasn't the only aspect. There were far greater ways of creating protections that she had learned. Rob had taught her how to mix the essences, but even without Rob's instructions, there were ways she had learned to protect herself.

Tessatha moved close to her, and she had her hands up. There was a streak of purple energy that worked out from her, a crackling of storm energy mixed with a deeper, almost grayish energy that came from the brambles as she built a layering of protection all around her. Serena had used flame and ice, a strange combination, but she had added earth in between it, mixing the three together to protect herself. She didn't know if it was going to be enough, but even as she was holding onto that power, she could feel some part of it that was building in a way that she thought she might be able to use.

"I've heard something like it before," Tessatha said.

"What is it?" Serena asked.

But they didn't have an opportunity to answer.

Three strange-looking birds came diving toward them.

They were pale gray, with massive, leathery wings, and small heads, but now they were filled with sharp fangs, and his stunted and twisted-looking arms and legs. They battered at the barriers.

Serena pushed upward with her protection, creating a barrier that she used to press up and away, thinking she might find some way to burn off these entities. She wasn't sure if these were alive or if they were merely constructs, but given that they were inside the tower that had simply appeared, the possibility that these were essence constructs was incredibly likely, more likely than having some creature that had lived here for a long period of time.

But the creatures ignored the boundary.

They began to press through.

One of them managed to get through the outer layer. That was mostly earth, mixed with a bit of ice, and Serena hurriedly added a bit of life essence, thinking about how Rob had described it as capable of devouring, but even that wasn't enough. She mixed water, then bramble and storm, before finally solidifying them in what was a makeshift form of unity, though the blending of power was not nearly as strong as what she thought it needed to be for her to overpower this.

She continued to press upward. An explosion of energy radiated outward. It came from Tessatha. The creatures were tossed upward but recovered to batter at the protection.

"I'm not sure how long we're going to be able to hold this," Tessatha said.

"You think that we can overpower them?"

"With what?" Tessatha asked. "I saw what you tried to do, and I tried to use storm and bramble, but it didn't have any effect on them."

"What kind of power do you think they have that they can ignore what we are doing?"

She arched a brow at her. "Unity, obviously. They are constructs; I suspect. And powerful."

"So, you think the tower is creating this?"

"I think the tower is creating all of this. Some of it might be defenses, and some of it might just be the tower's natural mechanism, but whatever it is, I think that we must be careful with it. I don't know how much we want to destroy, or we might have the tower attacking us even more."

The strange creatures continued to batter at the protections that they had formed, leaving Serena wondering if maybe there was going to be anything that she would be able to do. She tried to hold her barrier upward, but though she could access her essence and feel that power flowing through her, there did seem to be a limit to how much power she could draw. She had been summoning it, and holding onto it, with a burst of power and energy that she thought she might be able to maintain, but now...

Now it felt as if she were draining more and more with each passing moment. She tried to hold onto it and make sense of what was happening, but she could not.

"Okay," she said, looking over to Tessatha, "there's a problem here. I'm only going to be able to hold onto this for a little while longer, and I suspect, given the way that you look, that you're straining," she said, noticing the tension around Tessatha's eyes, but more than that, feeling some of the tension coming through the shared connection that the two had, a connection that had reformed the moment that they came into this room, which Serena had not even realized until now, "I think you're struggling, as well. So," Serena said, looking around. "The key here is trying to find a door. That is what we had to do in other places, and it seems that the tower wants us to find a door, so where is it here?"

"I haven't found anything," Tessatha said.

The inside of this room wasn't so large that they would be able to hide a door. There weren't any other items, unlike the last one, and it didn't seem as if anything along the walls would be useful as a door, so what were they going to find now?

She turned her attention to the floor, thinking that maybe there would be something like that there had been in the last space, but there was nothing. The stone was smooth and unremarkable. There was nothing about it that she thought she would be able to make sense of, and certainly nothing that would help them find their way to freedom.

Finally, she looked up.

She used a burst of fire and pressed through her boundary toward the shrieking birdlike creatures, but past them as well. She ignored their cries, and they mostly ignored the fire, as it didn't seem as if they were all that concerned about it, while she sent it blooming off toward the upper reaches of this room. She had known immediately when they came inside that it was a domed room, as they had enough light to make out the room's peak, though it was probably three stories above him. With the light radiating upward, it streaked along the walls, allowing her to see the contours of the stone and testing whether there were any higher-up doors, but she saw nothing there, either. Thankfully.

She started to pull her gaze away, turning back to Tessatha, when something glittered at the edge of her vision. She hadn't expected it, but as the bloom of fire she'd sent shooting upward had reached the room's peak, toward the dome itself, she saw an outline.

"What does that look like to you?" Serena asked softly.

She sent another pulse upward, past the birds, and urged it with an intensity that would hopefully overwhelm anything coming at them. By the time it reached the dome, Serena was certain of what she had seen. And her heart sank.

"It looks like a door."

The door was high overhead, above the birds trying to break through the protections that they had managed to secure, up near the dome itself, high enough that they would somehow have to get to the ceiling, and then fight through the creatures, for them to reach the door that was there.

But what was worse, is that there were at least three more of the birds perched around the door, as if defending it.

"How are we supposed to get past all of that?" Serena asked.

She didn't expect an answer.

Chapter Eighteen
SERENA

Serena focused on the creatures overhead, trying to figure out what they were going to need to do to get up to the door. That door loomed high above them, and even with the access to the essence she already had, she wasn't entirely sure what it was going to take for her to get past those creatures. The three attacking the barrier she and Tessatha had made only part of the challenge. There were three more up there that she wasn't sure they were going to be able to get past, but she knew that they were going to need to try to find some way to do so.

"Any suggestions?" Serena asked Tessatha.

"Not at this point," she said. "From what I can tell, these creatures seem to be focusing on the essence we are using, but I don't know if it is only about the essence, or if there is something else, we could use on them."

Using essence on these creatures seemed like a mistake, though it was the kind of mistake that Serena wasn't entirely sure that she had an answer for, anyway. It seemed to her that they were going to have to do something, but how were they supposed to get past it? Those creatures were circling in a way that left Serena... Uncomfortable.

It was the only way to describe it. She felt completely uncomfortable with what was happening and did not know what more they were going to need to do, but the essence around her was starting to pulsate again.

It had been doing that when it was time for them to leave the room. The unity essence continued to build and began to squeeze and constrict, giving her a distinct sense of energy coursing through her and making her feel as if she had no choice but to try to find a way out. It wasn't painful, not yet, but it was only a matter of time before it became that way.

"How long do you think we have?" Tessatha asked.

"You can feel it?"

"I'm starting to feel it," she said.

"Only a few minutes, I suspect."

Tessatha nodded, keeping her gaze locked overhead. Both were focused on it, though. The bird creatures started to batter at the essence again. Holding onto it was a challenge.

If they were to streak straight up, maybe they could reach that doorway in time to open it, but that involved getting past those birds. And Serena was not entirely sure they could do that very easily.

So, she readied herself.

The unity essence all around her began to constrict more than before, pressing through her. It was unpleasant. She felt it as a repercussion that seemed to work against her own natural essence. When she felt in the very first room, it had been a burning sort of pain, a compression. Then once she'd been in the other room, it had been a very different sort of sensation. Now...

Now it felt like there was a pressure that seemed to come from all around her, and it was difficult to get past it. She struggled, though she wanted to try to find some way to ignore it. She recognized the way that the essence was working inside of her, and she thought that maybe she would be able to use her own essence to counter it, but any time she attempted to do so, she could feel some part of it working against her. And from the way that she saw Tessatha's expression and the tightness in her eyes, she realized that she was also struggling.

"I think that we need to release our essence, and just go as quickly as possible," Serena said.

"It's dangerous," Tessatha said.

"What's the alternative?"

"One of us goes," Tessatha said.

Serena frowned. "I don't think that makes sense."

"And I think it does. We could have one draw off the creatures," she began, and from how she was saying it, Serena knew she wanted to sacrifice herself, "and we draw the creatures down to us. That gives the other of us an opportunity to reach the door and go through it. Then we can see what the tower wants of us."

Serena was shaking her head. "I'm not willing to do that. If we risk that, and if we go through, the only thing going to happen is that we are split up, and I think we need to be together to figure out what we must do here. We're stronger together."

That was something that she had learned from Rob. She didn't like it when she was separated from Rob, but then again, she had come to know that working together was much better than when they worked alone. Wasn't that going to be the key to all of this, anyway? Rob had been adamant that the essence they were working on, the power they were summoning, would be the key to everything they were doing. And if they could not figure out a way to work together, they would be divided, and the heralds, and whoever they served, would have an advantage over them.

"I think we need a sacrifice," Tessatha said.

"I think differently," Serena said, stepping over to Tessatha, and taking her hand. She let some of her essence flow, moving from her, and into Tessatha.

It was a different sort of sense than what she had before, as when she had been radiating out from her, she had been using it in an attack technique, but this was not any sort of an attack. This was merely a way of connecting to Tessatha and feeling a sense of reassurance to her. And she did. She appreciated the energy that came from her, the way Tessatha's essence began to build, and the connection she suddenly shared between them.

"We can do more when we stay together."

"It's just that—"

"I know what your experience has been," Serena said.

And to a certain extent, she did. She didn't really understand everything that Tessatha and the Netheral had gone through, but she knew they had sacrificed. If they were to keep doing that, sacrificing, then who was going to be lost this time? Tessatha? Then Arowend would be devastated again and might even need to try to find a way to gather her energies again, and maybe rebuild herself. Perhaps that was what Tessatha wanted. Allow her to become the same essence entity that Arowend had become. But Serena also thought there had to be another way for that.

And if it was Serena, then what would Rob do?

Those were the questions that she didn't have an answer to, as she understood how Rob would fight, and she understood that Rob would grow angry at what had happened.

No. It must be both of us.

But not because of what would happen to Arowend or Rob. Not because of what would happen to Serena and Tessatha. It had to be both of them because they were simply stronger together. They could find answers together.

She looked over to Tessatha and took her other hand. Once they did, essence flowed between them like it hadn't before. It seemed to build in ways that it had not done before.

Serena looked up and rapidly withdrew her barricade, telling Tessatha what she intended. The other woman nodded, and the two of them immediately began to streak upward.

Combined together, using the linked essence way that they did, they had more power than they would individually. Serena had known that such a thing was possible, as she had linked with others many times, and she understood that there was more that could be gained through such a linkage, but it had been a while since she had attempted to do something like that.

They passed beyond the first of the creatures. They darted toward them, but Serena and Tessatha were fast, the essence carrying them much more rapidly than they would've gone individually. They reached where the other three were, almost as if they were waiting. Serena focused upward, using a blast of combined essences, but not just combined essences from herself, but combined essence that was carried through her and Tessatha, linked together. If there were more of the dragon blood with them, then maybe they would've been able to have done even more.

They exploded upward, striking the space around the doorway.

It scattered the creatures.

They wouldn't have much time. And even as they reached the creatures, they were already starting to come back together, gathering near the doorway.

She focused on the symbols. "Do you see anything that you recognize?"

Tessatha nodded hurriedly. "There are a few."

Serena let her do the work, and activated the symbols, quickly causing the doorway to glow steadily. The creatures were battering at the protections that Serena and Tessatha had, but thankfully with their combined effort, they were strong enough not to overwhelm them. Then the door began to glow.

Serena let out a sigh of relief.

That was what they needed, wasn't it? They had to

focus together, they had to travel together, and they had to…

Power began to pull upon her.

She felt as if some part of her was getting ripped free.

At first, she was unsure of what it was, but it felt like the door, and its essences were trying to stripe some of her own essences.". Was it because she and Tessatha had been holding onto so much power? She didn't like that, but she wasn't about to release it, as the essence had been the key to what they were doing, and the only way that she thought that she might be able to survive this.

The door continued pulling upon her the same way it had in the other spaces. Serena let it draw her. She didn't fight, as she wasn't even sure that she would be able to fight. She felt the essence ripping through her and realized what was happening almost too late.

It was trying to tear her free from her connection to Tessatha.

She wasn't sure if she should let it go. Maybe that was what she needed to do at this point: release the link and satisfy whatever the tower wanted.

But then they were through.

The pressure upon her eased. There was no more of the unity, nothing that squeezed her. She was in a darkened space. She turned, immediately focusing on her essence, and found that while she had access to it inwardly, she found it difficult to express that externally.

"Tessatha?" Serena asked, turning and looking for her.

She saw no sign of her. There was no real light in the room, nothing she could feel, only an emptiness. Whatever had happened here, whatever had been done, had stripped Tessatha free from her.

Some part of that unity seemed as if it were signaling her.

Maybe it's guiding me toward Tessatha.

She had felt that drawing before, hadn't she?

When she had been outside of the tower, and when she had been dealing with the way that essence had been moving through the realms, she had noticed how it was flowing and had noticed that there was something more to it that she thought she might be able to use. So why shouldn't that essence guide her now? Serena had no reason to believe that it shouldn't be doing such a thing.

So, she focused. She couldn't see anything or feel any sign of Tessatha, but she had to believe that the tower itself was trying to tell her something. Maybe even guide her somewhere. That was what had been happening ever since she had entered the tower.

It seemed as if the tower had purposes for each of the rooms. This one was dark, but she didn't have the same sense of pressure as she had another one. When she reached the wall, she paused, running her fingers along the wall's surface, testing whether there was any marking within it, the same way that there had been markings on some of the other walls, working her way along until she reached an end. The room had to be over a hundred paces in one direction. And that was assuming that she had started from one end, which she wasn't entirely sure she had. She followed this wall and made it another hundred paces. How was it possible that the tower was this large? She had a hard time believing there was a room of this size, but then again, if all of this was some sort of essence construct, it could be.

The room's pressure began to build, much like it had every other time she had been in one of these rooms. It was starting to squeeze and constrict, power building through her. It was painful.

But the pain wasn't a problem, was it?

Rob helped her see that pain often meant change, and change could be positive.

Especially when it came to progression.

Was that what the tower was?

There was no sign of Tessatha.

She continued searching, but the essence was building beyond where Serena could withstand it. She dropped to her knees.

She crawled forward.

She collapsed, lying on the ground, when the pain became too much. That pain pulsated through her, pressing through her head and body.

What is it doing to me?

She tried to fight it, feeling as if everything within her wanted her to fight it, and her essence began to cry out. Fire bloomed inside of her in a way that it had not since she had been inside the tower. She had felt the fire and used it, but this time it seemed as if some part of her core began to blaze with the vibrant and burning intensity. Once it did, some of the other essences within her seemed to ignite, one after the other, the essence brightening with their intensity, and an awareness inside her that she thought she could use.

Serena got to her knees. She was able to move again,

thankfully, and she crawled forward, attempting to make her way toward the center of the room. She pushed out with a hint of light, that glowing energy radiating around her, and saw a doorway.

It was unlike any of the other doors that she had seen.

This one seemed freestanding in the center of the room, and once her light struck it, it bent around it, almost as if it could not penetrate fully into the doorway. She slowly dragged herself over to it. By the time she reached it, she had got to her feet and looked at the doorway. It was different on either side. One side had a series of symbols that were vastly different from the other. Serena didn't know which one the way was to go, but it did seem as if she was going to have to make a choice. When she did, she didn't know what she was going to find on the other side. The only problem that she had was that if she did activate the door, and if she did head through, then she was going to be leaving Tessatha behind.

And she didn't want to leave Tessatha behind.

But it didn't seem like the tower was giving her much choice. The tower had already separated them, stripping them free from each other. Serena couldn't even feel her, even with her essence now activated inside of her.

So, what choice did she have? The tower wanted them to go separate ways.

And maybe, this was a test. And if that were the case, the tower guided them where they needed to go.

She feared what sort of test she would encounter alone.

Chapter Nineteen
AROWEND

Arowend stood inside the tower. The room was strange, and it seemed to be made of crystalline walls, which reflected light all around him. He had expected darkness inside the tower, but there was nothing of the sort. The walls seemed to radiate their own light and energy coming off them, leaving him with a sense of the power that was here, but it was an unpleasant sort of sense.

He was aware of the unity, but then again, ever since Rob got into the nexus, and did whatever it was that he had done, Arowend was *always* aware of that unity. He couldn't help but feel it all around. It was not like the unity he had within himself or the kind of unity he thought he could manufacture inside of himself. That was artificial, he was aware. As much as he wanted that to be something real and powerful, Rob had proven just how different it was when a person had access to a different kind of unity.

And so, as he felt the unity around him, pressing inward, he recognized it for what it was. But none of that mattered to him.

He focused more on the physical form that he had. It reminded him of the form he had been taking on, but this was far more substantial. He couldn't transition, which felt strange given all the time that he had spent changing forms, floating from one to another, and growing accustomed to the fact that, as an essence entity, he was not confined to any specific physical form. To be honest, Arowend had come to like that. It made things much easier for him. But not only that, there was a certain freedom in it and trapped in this way, trapped in his body once again, he felt as if he lost some of that freedom again.

But perhaps he didn't. Perhaps he had been given something else, a gift or some way of trying to understand just what was out there, though Arowend didn't know if that was the case. He only knew he was inside the tower, and he now had to find Tessatha and Serena.

They needed help.

At least, that was what he believed, but now that he was here, he could feel the strange unity pressing upon him. He started to wonder if perhaps he was the one who needed help.

"What is it that you want of me?" Arowend asked.

He didn't expect an answer, but he asked it anyway. It felt as if the entity around him, the essence he felt around him, was powerful. But not only was it powerful, it felt as if it were a part of something greater.

It reminded him of what Serena had described the

palace as. He had never connected to that power, though he had previously known others who had.

Had I?

That thought was strange. He didn't remember having those memories, but perhaps he had known somebody with that kind of power, as it did seem to him that there would have to have been others connected to the different types of powers around him. And now…

Now he had to focus, and he thought about the palace, as that was the one that seemed to be driving some of the memories. Serena was connected to it, and he thought that perhaps with her connection, that maybe she would be able to help him understand more about the different types of essence, the energy, and the powers that existed in the world, but so far, he had only begun to learn about certain parts of it and had not been able to do all that much.

And perhaps that was not a problem for him.

He was different.

"You must move," a voice said, seemingly coming from all around him.

It was a female voice that was strange, commanding, and powerful.

Everything within Arowend went cold, almost as if this were some sort of God speaking to him.

Must he move?

"Move where?"

Who was he even talking to? And how was he talking to them? It didn't seem to be coming from a dragon mind connection, and he wasn't sure he heard it, so how were they speaking?

Essence.

That was the obvious answer, as the essence he felt around him continued to radiate with power, to the point where he could feel it vibrating. This other entity must be using essence in a way to speak to him that Arowend had never even considered. Was it possible for him to do something similar?

But didn't he already do that? He was using essence to communicate across great distances already, using the dragon mind connection that bridged him to others, including Rob, Tessatha, Serena, and any others who wanted and were willing to speak to him. Why should there be any other way for this power—and the tower was obviously some sort of power—to be able to speak to him?

Arowend looked around. How was he supposed to move from here?

The room was small. Probably only a few paces in either direction, with crystalline walls that seemed to reflect essence back at him. He saw his reflection, though it was twisted and contorted, making it seem like he was twisted and contorted within it. Almost as if the crystals themselves were trying to trap him.

Not the crystals. The essence.

As he focused on it, he was aware of the essence within those. He couldn't see it, but he could definitely *feel* it. And his own essence…

His own essence was different than it had been before. Arowend could feel the way it was coursing through him, filling his body in a way he had not felt in a long time. And perhaps that was the challenge. He had not been accustomed to having a body need essence, to change it, to contort it, and to require the power flowing through him. But now that he was there, he could feel the way that essence pumped with his heart, how it flowed out to his skin, how it worked its way down into his mind, down inside some core part of him.

Had the tower given him a body once again? And if it had, was this permanent?

He had not remembered the way it felt. And maybe that was a problem. He had been diffused for too long. And he didn't mind it, because that diffusion had allowed him to do things that others could not, but having a body, and feeling the power that he now did, left him wondering whether there was something else for him, something more that he might be able to uncover, something that would help him understand his own essence, and what was going to take for him to progress, in ways that he had not attempted to learn in quite some time. The more he could feel it, the more he began to recognize the essence coursing through him, and the more he felt aspects of him awakening that had been lost for longer than Arowend could remember.

And he *did* remember.

He had allowed himself to forget.

But some of it had been stripped away, shattered during his destruction, but some of it was always there. And that was what Arowend needed to find now. He had to understand what the essence was trying to tell him.

He focused on it. There was a certain pulsation around him, something that he could feel from the unity, and yet, there was some part of it that left him feeling uncomfortable. That was new, as the unity itself shouldn't be uncomfortable to him, but the longer that he focused on what he could feel, the more certain he was that power that he detected was pressing through him, and trying to work against him, in a way that left him radiating danger.

What would Rob do?

He pushed those thoughts aside. Why was he thinking about Rob in this situation?

Rob would not have gotten trapped like this. Rob would've been able to use the unity, and probably would've known what to do with the tower in the first place. Rob would have known all these things.

Arowend did not.

But that didn't mean that he was any less than Rob.

He was different. *Was that a bad thing?*

He tried not to think about the comparison, but everything he had done with Rob and everything he had experienced seemed tied to him ever since Rob's appearance. And as much as that seemed strange, he was thankful for it, as well. Were it not for Rob, and everything he would've done, Arowend would've been trapped as the Netheral.

You must move.

Those thoughts came back to him, almost as if the entity of the tower was speaking to him again, but Arowend wasn't sure how he was going to move. There wasn't any way for him to leave this space.

He started forward, though. It felt weird for him to walk, at least weird with him once again inside of a body, and trying to move as if he were alive, but at the same time, he felt as if it were something he needed to do.

That power was there, pressing through him, and extending outward. Essence flowed within him. He was moving.

When he reached the crystalline wall, he reached out for it. His sense of touch had changed ever since he had been an essence form. He found it different for him, difficult for him, to try to understand the power that was here, and though he was reaching out for the wall, trying to test whether there was anything that he might be able to determine, he wasn't sure what it was that he found. Power, perhaps.

The crystals glowed beneath his hand.

And more than that, he felt the sense of unity that was there. There was power.

That power seemed to emanate from him, emanate into him, and it seemed to echo with some part of him. He wasn't sure what that was, or what it meant, only that he could feel some part of it seeming to react.

He traced his hand along the crystals, running his fingers through them until he found an area that felt a little different. There was pain, but Arowend had grown accustomed to pain over time, and it no longer bothered him. He was only distantly aware of it. The only thing that he was certain of was that the unity was compressing down upon him. It seemed to be coming from all around, as if the crystals surrounding him were concentrating that power and trying to focus it upon him. That didn't bother him, though. As he could feel it, and he could feel the way that power was radiating, and he could feel it compressing his essence.

Odd. The unity was active against him.

Was that what Tessatha and Serena had experienced?

If it were only him here, Arowend thought that he would've taken the time to wander and try to make sense of what he felt, but even as he did now, he wasn't sure that there was anything here that he would be able to identify. But he knew that if he were to linger and the others were here, experiencing the same sort of thing, they might not be as accustomed to the pain as he was.

And he didn't want them to suffer.

Tessatha had suffered enough.

Serena had suffered enough, and Arowend was responsible for some of that. He wasn't going to do anything that would make them suffer anymore. He needed to try to help them, and he needed to try to find some way to do so. He worked his way around the wall and found himself back in the center, still feeling that power around him.

That power continued to constrict. He remembered something along the lines of this, though he wasn't sure where it had been. It had concentrated down upon him. The power that had focused on him, the power that had built, rose within him while Arowend attempted to counter it.

That was a new memory.

Countering it.

There is only one thing he could have thought would be like that, which was tied to what happened to him. The idea that the attack would come back to him now, after all this time, was terrifying. Why fill his mind now? Why would there be memories of what had happened, what he had experienced, and what he had become?

But he remembered.

The power that had targeted him had held him in place. Arowend had not been able to move, though he had strained to do so. He remembered the faces of each of them. They were powerful. They had access to different essences, much like he did, and though he had been trying to reach for a power that he believed existed in the land, something that he thought would unite all their lands in a natural form, they had feared it.

And they had trapped him.

Linking around him.

It was the only way that they would've been able to overpower him.

Not because Arowend was necessarily more powerful than them, but because they had access to much more when they were united than they did apart, which was the very lesson he had been trying to get across to them. If they understood that linking would help protect them, why could it not help protect their land? That was the hard part for him, as he could not convince them otherwise, even though he had continued to try to do so. But then they had surrounded him. It was a simple place, a plain outside each of their realms, and a place where Arowend had started to search for the energy that he knew existed. He had found all signs pointing toward something real, but they had not wanted him to do that. They had feared what he might uncover. They had feared losing what they already had.

More than that, they feared what was coming.

Arowend had recognized that there was something else out there that required greater strength, but they had feared what it would do. And he had known that there was good reason for them to fear. How could he not, as he had detected something more?

When they linked around him, they connected to the greater power.

And then they focused on him.

He remembered the tearing. He remembered... the pain that was much like what he felt now.

Was that happening to him again?

Was the tower itself trying to tear him apart?

Arowend roared. "Why are you doing this to me?"

"You must move," the tower answered, almost immediately.

Move? How was he supposed to move? Where was he supposed to move?

And yet, he was more aware of the pain he'd been feeling and the way it was working through him than he had been in quite some time. Arowend wanted nothing more than to move, to rip his way through the tower, to get his vengeance for what had happened to him. That was what he wanted, as he had suffered.

They had done that to him.

No. Not the tower. The others.

He called himself.

It took a great effort of will for him to do that, as Arowend had struggled with that for far too long. Ever since he had returned to some semblance of awareness, he had still struggled with it. He had been something else. He had been Arowend but also tried to refuse the Netheral.

But he was both. Wasn't he?

The Netheral represented his anger at what happened; there was no reason for him to deny that. There was every reason for him to accept the fact that he was angry, and he was angry for good reason. What happened to him was horrifying and should not have happened. It should not happen to any others, but it had happened to him.

Arowend raged; this time, he didn't fight the rage within him. He accepted it, and he acknowledged it, and he did not mind the fact that it was there within him.

But he kept it a part of himself. As he did, the essence within him seemed to bloom.

It was almost as if he had been restricting himself, not so much the tower.

And then he saw something along that crystal starting to shift.

He started toward it, and Arowend exploded power out from him with a burst of the essence. He shattered the crystal, which dissolved in a glimmering light, fading into a little more. Unity essence. He supposed he should have been impressed by that, but he was not. Instead, Arowend was annoyed.

Move.

Where was he supposed to go?

Now that the crystals were gone, and the limit on him had been lifted, he strode forward, into the darkness of the tower. But he didn't see anything else.

The only thing he saw was darkness.

How was he supposed to find them?

Essence filled him, though. It had taken a while for it to return to him, but now that it did, he was aware of something else. He had this physical form, something that the tower had demanded that he possessed, forcing it down upon him, but the physical form wasn't him any longer. Arowend knew that, as he could be something *more*. He didn't mind this physicality, but having the memory of it gave him an opportunity to know just what he once had been, but now he was something else. He was an essence entity.

And he took advantage of that, focusing on the essence within him, and then he exploded outward.

It was almost as if he tore free of his physical form, though that wasn't quite right. The physical form was still there if he were to manifest it, and now that he remembered what it had been like and how it felt, he thought he could re-create it much better than he had before. But for now, none of that mattered. The only thing that mattered was that he was free.

And now that he was free, he was going to find Tessatha. He was going to find Serena.

And he was going to get them out of this tower.

Chapter Twenty

SERENA

S̃ERENA COULDN'T SEE ANYTHING.

Each room seemed to be the same. Each time that she passed through one doorway, into another, she felt as if she were entering another world. And maybe that was part of it. As she passed through, heading from one place to the next, she could feel that energy changing within her, some part of her that was modified by what was there, and she could feel some part of it that existed that made it so that she could not do much of anything. She had to reorient to her essence, trying to make sense of it and feel how her essence was permitted in each space. And it did seem as if she had to wait for it to be permitted. The tower gifted, but it also seemed to take away.

What was here now?

The walls were different. They had a gentle slope, with a bit of curvature, and within them, she saw…

She wasn't sure what she saw, only that she felt some part of the unity here. The tower kept moving her through it as if it were trying to funnel her, but that following seemed to guide her someplace else, someplace that would have more power. And every single moment that passed, she could feel some part of that power pressing upon her in a way that Serena felt as if she had to understand better so that she could know what was happening to her. The tower wanted something.

And why had she not attempted to speak to it if it wanted something? That was an odd thought, but then again, she had spoken to other different entities, hadn't she?

And she had been aware that the palace, and some other places, had also been incredibly powerful. Why could it not be the tower? And if the tower were powerful, then Serena would have no reason to believe that the tower should not be able to work with her, and try to answer her questions so that she might be able to understand what was here, and what she might be able to find.

"What are you trying to do with me?"

She spoke aloud, and yet, she did more than that. As she spoke, she focused on the essence within her, and she tried to radiate some of that outward so that she might be able to let it flow in a way that the tower itself might recognize. She could feel it and some part of herself reacting, even if she wasn't entirely sure what was happening to it.

In the last space, she had exploded fire within her, and it had burned off whatever the tower was trying to do to her. It had awoken the other essences, and now they were still there so that Serena didn't have to feel like she couldn't use her essence as she was supposed to. That access was still within her.

"You obviously want me to do something. I need Tessatha. Don't keep her from me."

She felt ridiculous saying that much, but at the same time, she wanted her friend back. She didn't want the tower to keep them separated.

"The journey is yours," a voice said.

It was a deep, rich, female voice. At least that's what she thought; Serena wasn't entirely sure. A part of her was left thinking it reminded her a bit of her mother; only her mother would never have spoken to her like that.

Or would she?

Maybe this was all a trick? She had no idea what was happening around her, only that there was power. Was it the tower speaking to her, or was it some reflection of essence that was manifesting?

Anything was possible in a place like this. The power was significant and potent, making it so that Serena could not even know what she was dealing with. The energy of the unity was far beyond her understanding, and perhaps she could not fully understand what was happening, nor the way that it was working around her. Not without having time to sit and study. But without having access to the unity, she may not be able to understand it.

"The journey is mine, but I don't have to walk alone," Serena said. She looked up, but she couldn't see anything. It was almost as if there was a bit of a haze over her, like a cloud.

"You have to know, Rob. He has been walking this journey with me."

At the mention of Rob, she felt…

Serena wasn't entirely sure what it was that she felt. Maybe the conduit reacted. It had been a while since she had felt anything through that conduit, almost as if Rob were trying to stay distant, though she doubted that was the case. Ever since she had come into the tower, it had severed some aspect of the connection, making it so that she could not reach for him. She believed that he was still there, and she was so connected to him, but without having enough access, she wasn't sure she would be able to do much more with it.

"The journey is yours," the voice said again.

Serena smiled to herself. That suggested that this was a construct, and it was repeating certain phrases that it thought it needed.

But what if it wasn't?

The idea that this could be something real, and that there could be some real power here, left her…

Well, it left her feeling uncertain. If the tower was aware in any way, Serena thought that she would need to try to understand better why, and what it meant. The tower certainly had continued to expand and grow. Something that had simple constructs generally didn't do, though maybe it wasn't a simple construct. Over time, the essence around her had continued to expand, fill, and flow, leaving her thinking that perhaps there had to be some other way to understand it.

"Let me find a Tessatha," she said.

"The journey is yours."

Serena started to smile to herself. The journey was hers. Of course, it was. But somehow, she was going to need to use her essence...

Her essence.

She had an essence, didn't she? In the last room, Serena had focused on her essence, and she allowed that power to bloom within her, and the tower hadn't severed it quite the same way it had before. Now that Serena could feel the essence, she felt some part of her reacting, radiating that power, and accepting the energy flowing within her. She thought that it might be useful to her and that maybe if she drew upon what she felt, she could reach for Tessatha.

She didn't think she would be able to reach for Rob, as the tower had severed that connection for whatever reason, but Tessatha was inside the tower.

She closed her eyes and focused on the dragon mind connection she shared with Tessatha. Had she not had as much time as she had with Tessatha exploring, trying to understand the world around her, she wasn't sure she would've been able to feel for her now. But she and Tessatha had become friends. They had become close. And because of that, Serena could feel something that she had not been able to feel otherwise. She recognized that Tessatha had a presence there. It was diffuse and hazy, but it was definitely there. The more she focused on what she felt, the more she began to recognize that Tessatha was there, the more she started to pull upon it, and then...

And then she felt a connection form.

"Tessatha," she said, using the dragon mind connection.

There was a moment of silence, and then Tessatha's mind connected to Serena. "Are you out?"

"I'm in some massive room. I don't know where it is, only that I barely survived the last one."

"I had to face some constructs," Tessatha said.

"You had to fight?"

"They tried to surround me. It reminded me of the brambles."

"I'm sorry," Serena said.

"I'm sorry I wasn't there with you."

"I can feel you," Serena said. "And…" As she closed her eyes and focused, she realized that there was something else as well. It wasn't what she had expected. But it was a familiar essence she had not expected to feel here. She detected it all around her, and there were tendrils of it that were close. "Is it Arowend with you?"

"Arowend? He's outside of the tower."

"I feel some part of him."

"I haven't managed to connect my essence quite as well," Tessatha said. "I'm surprised you have done this much."

"It's not so much that I did it, as I think I refuse to have the tower harm me. I could feel what was doing, and fought through it until fire blazed within me."

"Something similar happened to me," she said, and a series of images came to Serena. She appreciated the dragon mind ability, and how they could communicate so much more effectively using images, not requiring that they speak and communicate in that manner. Serena saw what looked like thick vines of power that stretched, straining toward Tessatha, until Tessatha had drawn upon her own connection to the bramble essence, something that Serena still didn't fully understand. It shattered the attack that was coming at her. The combination was significant, and finally, Tessatha had reached her own essence, until she found a door wrapped in branches. And then...

"Wait," Serena said.

She sent a burst of glowing light outward from herself. When she did, she saw a darkened figure on the far side of the room.

She snorted.

"It seems as if we're in the same place," she said.

Tessatha turned to her, and she came running across the distance until she reached Serena. Tessatha was filled with her own essence, primarily the bramble essence, though the others were also active and alive within her. Much like Serena had her own essence active and alive within her, Tessatha swept her gaze around her, looking up, and her gaze lingered on the ceiling as if there was going to be something up there that they might be able to find. Serena had felt something there, though she wasn't sure what it was, and she knew that they weren't going to be able to uncover it without trying to use essence. They could link. Now that they were here together, they might be able to find their way out.

The last time they linked essence together, it seemed as if the tower was disappointed in what they had done, so maybe linking was not the right strategy.

"You said you felt Arowend?"

Serena nodded. "Can you?"

"As I said, everything feels…" She closed her eyes, and when she did, she began to focus on her essence. Serena could see it within her, the way that it was rising within her, doing much more than it had before. Finally, Serena felt as if she were gaining access to power in the way that it had before. She had not known anything quite like that since entering the tower. It was almost as if some part of the tower had stripped away her abilities from her, only for her to regain them gradually.

But then again, Serena wanted more than just her previous abilities. She wanted to be able to do what Rob could do. And she increasingly thought that the tower was designed to help with that, even if she didn't know what it was, nor did she know how it would she wished that those answers would come to her, but it felt as if the tower were trying to fight her, to strip away everything that she could do, and to change things so that Serena could not progress.

"He's there," Tessatha said.

"You have a connection to him. Call him to you."

"I don't know if the tower works like that."

"This is Arowend," Serena said.

When Tessatha looked over, Serena shrugged.

Arowend was different. Maybe the tower wouldn't work the same way for him, but she also had a hard time thinking that Arowend would be trapped in the same way as they were. He could transition to his essence form, and ideally, he'd be able to travel through the tower, reach them, and then could he help them escape.

Serena wasn't quite sure if that was what she wanted

or not, but increasingly, she thought that she needed to try to find any other way to escape she could. The tower was holding onto them, and there was too much danger here for them to stay. If they found a way out, then they had to take it.

When Rob returned, they could come back, and see what he might be able to uncover. She hated that she relied upon Rob, but this was the kind of essence with which Rob had much more experience and understanding.

"He's there," she said, and she turned, looking around her. "But I can't quite reach him."

"Call to him," Serena said.

"I think we both need to."

Serena shook her head. "I have a feeling that when we link, it upsets the tower. That was the time when the tower stripped us apart. I don't know if we want to do that again."

"You think we *angered* the tower?"

Serena shrugged. "Well, it's really the only thing I can think of, as it makes a certain sort of sense."

Tessatha frowned. "You might be right. I hadn't thought about that."

Serena could feel for Arowend, but even as she did, she wasn't sure if what she felt was real or not. She could feel some of that power, and she could feel the way that it was radiating, and she could feel…

She wasn't entirely sure what she felt, only that she realized that there was some part of it there, something that suggested to her that Arowend was out there, maybe just beyond their reach.

Perhaps they could strain for him, and perhaps they could find some way to connect to him, but for now, she wasn't sure that it was going to make a difference.

Tessatha closed her eyes again.

And as she did, Serena wondered if there might be something more that they could learn. But even as they did, she began to wonder if the tower would limit them.

The haze over them continued to swirl, and then something about it began to change. Serena wasn't sure what it was, only that it began to shift, swirling gradually, and she noticed some other part of it drifting.

That was unusual. That was unexpected.

"Arowend," Serena said.

Then he formed.

When he did, he took on a much more substantial form than she remembered. It was almost as if he were able to take on that form, and he solidified in a way that gave him deeper features, wrinkles around the corners of his eyes, almost an intensity to his presence that had not been there before. Serena couldn't help but feel the intensity and the presence as if he were truly there. She marveled at it.

"There you are," he said, hurrying over to Tessatha, and wrapping her in a tight hug. Power emanated from him, swirling away, until it looped around Tessatha, mingling with her own essence. Serena looked away, as this felt far too personal, and she didn't want to have anything to do with it.

They whispered something softly to each other, though she wasn't sure if it was spoken aloud, or if it came through the essence. Whatever it was, Serena could feel some part of its beginning to bubble, and she recognized that it worked against him in ways that she had not felt before.

"How did you get here?" Tessatha asked.

Arowend looked around. "I came because I felt something. Your father," he said, nodding to Serena, "said that he was outside when the tower swallowed you. I knew that I needed to do something. I wasn't sure what I would be able to do, if anything, but I had to try."

"It's dangerous," Tessatha said.

"I've felt that."

"Are you able to travel freely?" Serena asked.

"Not entirely," he said. "When the tower first took me in, it forced me into this form." And by saying it, Serena had a feeling that it was the only form he could take other than his insubstantial one. That was odd, but Arowend didn't go on about it, so she didn't bother to press. "I found my way through essence and managed to escape."

"Something is different about you," Tessatha said.

Serena felt it, as well. It was more than just his form. While he was more substantial, it did seem as if something else about Arowend had changed. She wondered what it was. Had he found a way to use the essence better than they had?

She understood that Arowend had been trying to understand the unity, doing the same thing they were doing. He and Tessatha had been doing it for many years, so it wouldn't be terribly surprising to her if Arowend had uncovered something to help him master that aspect, but she would be disappointed if he had done it and had not shared that.

"I can feel it, as well," Arowend said. "I haven't progressed if that is your concern."

"I think the tower could help us," Serena said. When Tessatha looked at her, frowning, Serena shrugged. "Well, if we were able to understand it. I feel like all this unity essence is here and seems to be trying to tell us something. I don't even know what it is."

"Maybe it's just trying to test us," Tessatha said. She looked over Arowend. "That is how it has felt. What has it felt like to you?"

A troubled look crossed over his features. And then he forced a smile. "The same."

"What did you find?" Tessatha asked.

He shook his head. "It doesn't matter."

"It does. You remembered something."

His face fell. "I remembered what happened. I remember the way that they shattered me. I remembered how they used their essence, linked together, and how they destroyed me."

"Oh," Tessatha said softly. "I'm so sorry."

"I needed to remember," he said. "I feel like... I feel like I have been incomplete, unable to remember something pivotal to who I am and what I've become. And now they remember..." He shrugged. "I hope that I can move on. I hope that others can allow me to move on."

He watched Serena as he said it.

But Serena knew that it wasn't upon her to decide if he was going to be able to move on from what happened to him, and the others he had harmed. That wasn't her choice to make. She had forgiven him, as much as she could forgive him. That didn't mean that she liked what he had done or cared for the measures he had taken. In fact, Serena felt as if everything he had done had been much worse than what she would have. She and Rob had spoken about what might've happened if it had been the reverse, if it had been her, and Rob who had been destroyed in such a manner. What would've happened to them?

She liked to think that they wouldn't have taken the same action, but maybe it wasn't Arowend who had taken that action. Maybe it was some part of his essence, some part that was not really him, that had reacted in a way that had not known how to do anything else. And that made it hard for her to know whether they would have done something similar.

"Do you have any idea about how to get out?" Serena asked Arowend.

"I have searched the tower. I haven't found any doorways unless they present themselves."

"We must find a doorway to escape," Serena said.

And as she said it, she began to feel the essence around her beginning to bubble and build, the same way as it had every other time. Now that it was working against her, she realized that essence was rising faster than before. They weren't careful, and it was going to become too much for them.

But there was no sign of a doorway here.

At least they weren't alone.

That thought gave her some measure of peace, but it still wasn't enough.

"How do you find these doorways?" Arowend asked.

"They sort of appear," Tessatha said. "But we haven't been so good about finding them as they are about finding us."

"I fear we must work quickly," Arowend said.

Serena nodded. "The moment the essence begins to build like this, we have no choice but to move."

"That is not quite what I was suggesting," Arowend said, and then he pointed.

Serena saw other figures approaching them in the distance, to the room's far end. They seemed to be built of the essence, like the strange birds had been built of the essence, and they were moving quickly. Constructs.

And it seemed as if the tower had decided to attack.

Chapter Twenty-One

ROB

Rob could feel the energy around him.

"I think it's time for us to go," Alyssa said, looking over to Rob. "Unless you want to be here when the heralds come..."

"I think we have to work quickly now," Rob said, focusing below. He could feel the essence and that there was something there, some answer that he had to uncover. He could feel the essence there, the way it was connected to Alyssa and the others with her, some part of it bridging them, linking to them, in a way he had not seen before.

But now he could feel it. It was not *his* essence.

"There's power below," Rob said, looking at Alyssa. "Can you see it?"

"The only thing I can see is several subheralds and heralds coming at us. I think we don't want to be here," she said, looking at the others arranged around her. "This is more than we've ever faced before. We know the danger, Rob. And we know there are certain things we can do and certain things we cannot. You're trying to push us into something we cannot do."

"What if you can progress?"

She hesitated before answering, her voice quavering a moment. "What if we can… Do you think it's possible?"

Rob shrugged. "I don't know. I'm still trying to understand what is here, but I can feel something." And yet, what he was able to feel was not similar to the nexus.

But would it be?

He had experienced a combined power blended from all his realm's energy in the Nexus. What he was focusing on now would be the combined energy of *this* realm.

"Focus," he said.

"Rob," Alyssa said, and there was a note of fear in her voice that hadn't been there before.

Rob understood it. They were afraid, and for a good reason. They had barely survived several subheralds, and now they had heralds coming for them?

"I know," he said. "But if you do this, and if you progress, then we have the strength that they do not. We will be able to do things that they cannot. We will be able to counter what they cannot. We *need* you to progress."

"Why me? Why us? Why not you?"

It was the same question that Rob had been getting ever since he had started to chase progression on his own. He had always been willing to help others, wanting to help raise the people around him, partly because they also needed to gain power. He couldn't be the only one who progressed, as Rob understood that for him to have the kind of power he wanted, and for the people around him to have what he wanted and the safety that they wanted, they were going to need to all be more potent. And some had been far more accepting of it than others. Some had recognized that Rob had done so out of a desire for safety, while others still didn't believe. They feared that he was going to gain something of his own out of it.

And perhaps he did. With every person that progressed, Rob felt a greater connection to his own realm, and his world, in such a way that he felt like he could continue to use that knowledge, and that experience, so that he might be able to do more.

And he had.

Had it not been for the dragon blood, Rob wouldn't have been able to become what he was now. And so, it was for them, and the realm, but it was indirectly for Rob.

"We need to be able to fight," Rob said. "And I can't do it all. I'm happy to progress. If we learn anything with your progression, I will happily take on some aspect of that, but in this case, I don't know that I will. But I want you to be stronger so that you can defend yourself, and your people, against what is out there. And ideally, I want you to reclaim your realm. Your *true* realm."

He looked down, and as he did, he could feel the essence and see aspects of it moving beneath him, something that seemed as if it were blending together. That was the key if only he could make sense of it.

"What do I need to do?"

Rob smiled to himself. *This might work.*

"In my land, there was a place of power." He started sharing with her what he had experienced, and he started to tell her about the unity, and how the nexus had helped with it. The power of the realm below him was not as potent as it would've been in his land, but maybe it didn't need to be. Maybe once they started to push essence outward, they could blend it in a way that would build power more rapidly than it had before. Or perhaps it wasn't even possible. Rob didn't know.

"There's a place like that," she said. "A place that was always sacred, but most never really understood it. And yet, I don't know what we can do with it."

"I could go with you," he said.

She watched him.

"I won't be able to use your essence," he explained. "And I am not interested in trying to take your essence. I think that should be quite clear now."

"Clear, but still unsettling."

"Just show me," he said.

He paused to see what was coming. They might not have enough time if they did this before trying to retreat. If he could reach his border, he thought he could secure it against the subheralds, Rob had already seen how the border wouldn't hold back one of the heralds. And if they had more than one of the heralds, then it might be too much for him to handle.

And if the heralds all attacked, what would Rob do?

He would have to fight, but he wasn't sure that he or his allies were strong enough.

That was why he was selfishly pushing Alyssa and these others to progress. If they could become more than dragon blood and find some way to understand the unity, he had to believe they could do much more than they already had.

That was what he was after now.

Alyssa dropped toward her land.

Rob followed. The others joined them, descending, though there was hesitancy to them. Rob understood. How many had not returned to this land in a long time? Many of them might not even feel as if it were safe to return. And to a certain extent, it probably *wasn't* entirely safe, as there was little essence here for them to use. That essence had been drained away, leaving only faint tendrils of energy that lingered, but those faint tendrils were enough, from what Rob could tell.

Then they landed.

It was a barren black rock. There was no sign of life. No sign of grass, trees, flowers, ice, or brambles for lightning. Nothing that Rob had come to know as vibrancy and life of his realm was. Everything had been drained.

But not everything.

There was still that sense of essence, though it was faint and distant, enough so that as Rob attempted to try to make sense of it, he couldn't tell quite clearly enough.

"Now what?" Alyssa asked.

The others around them were circling, having not come to a complete standstill. It was almost as if they were afraid to land and come here. And maybe they were.

"Now we find a way to it."

"How?"

This came from one of the others, though Rob couldn't tell who it was. He didn't know the names of all of them, but he recognized the uncertainty and that they simply wanted answers.

"We have to manifest." He looked over to Alyssa. "You can't take your physical form with you. Where we are heading, if this is anything like it was in my realm, it is a place of incredible power. But it is a place your body cannot be."

"It will leave us exposed," she said, looking up at the sky. "We don't have much time."

"Then we must act quickly," Rob said.

When he had been dealing with the ice king, then the Nethcral, Rob had thought that he would eventually be able to bring about a measure of peace, but once they had uncovered the Eternal, and the other threat, it had felt as if everything were building against them with such intensity and such power that he was scarcely able to do much about it. Even now, Rob wasn't sure that it was going to be enough. He wasn't sure that *he* could be enough.

Alyssa nodded. "How do we find it?"

"I can help guide," he said. "Follow me."

And he realized he trusted them as much as they trusted him. He put himself in danger by leaving his physical form, at least mostly.

But he manifested and strained, heading down toward where he felt that bubbling of power. It was deep beneath the ground, drawing to him, but something about it was also familiar to him. Rob had experienced something like this before that reminded him of the nexus. He began to feel manifestations joining him. He was distantly aware of him and made a point of stretching out with his essence to guide them. Finally, he reached a cavern deep beneath the ground, much like the cavern in his realm.

It was a place of power. Even now, with every bit of essence stripped away from these realms, Rob could feel that about it.

Now that he was here, the others joined him. One by one until they were all here. Some were stronger, their manifestations far clearer, but they all appeared.

Alyssa stood at the edge of the nexus, as Rob suspected it was a nexus, and looked down. "How is something like this even possible?"

"I don't know," Rob said. "It's an ancient power. At least, it was ancient power in my realm. I suspect you had something similar."

"We always knew there was something, as we could feel it, but we weren't sure what it was. And now…"

"Now you need to go into it," Rob said.

Alyssa looked over. "I need to do what?"

"You must go into it. It is an essence, and you must use it."

"To do what? Drain it from these lands? I thought—"

"We are not going to drain it from your land," Rob said. He looked at each of the others, most of them silent as they approached the nexus, looking down upon it as if they were trying to decide whether it was any sort of danger to them. Or perhaps it wasn't just that they were looking down to see if it was a danger, more that they were looking down to see if they might be able to draw upon it. He couldn't tell. Many of them seem filled with a certain tension, which Rob knew all too well. Having experienced a nexus like this, and knowing that such power existed, he felt as if it could be terrifying. "What you're going to do is you're going to push the essence back into your land."

Alyssa looked over. "That's how they drained it the last time."

"They didn't drain it," Rob said. "They tried to. I don't even know if they understand the nexus." Rob wasn't entirely sure, as he didn't know the purpose of it, only that something had happened in his realm, and obviously, in Alyssa's realm, that had caused it to withdraw to a place like this. The people who lived in these lands, much like he did, had known about the power and had been aware of how they could draw upon it. He had to believe that was significant. "What you need to do is push it out. When you do, some part of you is going to change. At least, that was what it was like for me. I don't know if you can all be a part of the change, though," Rob said, looking at the others. "Or if it is only one who can benefit."

"What if it doesn't work like that here?" Alyssa asked.

"Then... I don't know."

"You go," Torrence said, an older man who had been traveling with Alyssa for a long time. "If anybody should do this, it should be you."

"It should be the oldest," Alyssa said.

"It should be the strongest," others said.

Alyssa hesitated. There was no doubting who the others meant. Alyssa *was* the strongest of them.

She looked over to Rob. "I'm afraid."

"Yes. But you should do it."

Distantly, Rob was aware of what was happening. He could feel the subheralds, and the onslaught of power getting closer to them. If Alyssa didn't do this, they were going to have to withdraw and either run or fight. And even if they were to run, they may still have to fight.

Alyssa dropped.

Rob was thankful when she did, as he hadn't been sure if she was going to take the plunge. As soon as she started to descend, he felt something. It was almost as if there were an echoing. Power seemed to hammer, swirling around, and building. There was some part of it that sent Rob teetering, and it took every bit of his own concentration for him to be able to focus on what was happening. He maintained a connection to Alyssa, knowing that Arowend had done the same to him and that it wouldn't make any change for him during the progression if the progression worked for her.

Awareness of her bloomed in his mind. He could see what she could see. She was trapped in the nebulous power, the energy swirling around her radiating outward, and yet, a part of Alyssa was trying to draw some of it into herself.

"Be careful," Rob cautioned, as he didn't know what would happen if she were to try to draw that power into herself. Maybe it would be too much, but more likely, and it would simply make the plan that they had failed. And he could tell that she did not want to fail.

"It's so much," she breathed out.

"And not enough," Rob realized. "You need to speak to the others. They must give up their realms."

"What are you talking about?"

As he focused, he could feel that something was missing. The power that had been drawn away and restricted and that had been isolated limited what could happen here. And if they did not give up those realms, Rob wasn't sure that this was even going to work. The realms of this place needed to have more power. They needed to have the essence, and they needed to have the potential for them to focus and link that power together.

Would they even be willing to do it?

Rob couldn't tell, but it wasn't even for him to do so. It wasn't for him to be the one to tell them that they needed to do this. It wasn't for him to do anything. It was for Alyssa. These were her people. This was her power. This was her realm. If she did it, and it worked, she would have access to unity. If she didn't...

They never would, Rob suspected.

"Feel what the nexus is giving you," he said. "Because I know you can. It is all around you. Feel what it's trying to tell you. Feel that energy and feel what you need to do."

There was a moment of silence, and then Alyssa seemed to recognize what he was telling her. More than that, there was the energy radiating out from her, that was straining, stretching, and flowing in a way that it had not before.

She was pushing on the nexus here.

But even as she did, it was not flowing as it should.

"If this doesn't work, we will lose everything."

"And if it works, you will gain more than you can imagine."

He felt Alyssa connecting to him, and he felt the fear within her, and then he heard her call to the others.

Rob waited, not knowing what they would decide.

Chapter Twenty-Two

SERENA

Serena looked at the oncoming creatures making their way toward her and the others, not quite sure what to do. The essence had not been enough when they had dealt with the creatures before. At that point, she had access to enough of her essence that she thought she should have been able to counter what was coming, but now she wasn't quite sure if such a thing would even be possible.

The kind of power she felt coming toward her now was considerable. And, more than anything else, it struck her as reminiscent of unity.

Of course, it would. The unity essence that was coming at them was tied to the tower. That unity essence was all around, and it continued to swirl and press down upon her.

"I can take care of them," Arowend said.

Serena shook her head. "I don't know that you can. And, more than anything else, I don't know that you *should*. We aren't entirely sure what we're dealing with, only that it is tied to the palace in some way. And…"

More and more, she thought that the key was going to be trying to find a way to work with what the palace wanted.

"What do you want from us?" Serena asked.

Tessatha looked at her, and there was a question in her eyes; there was a question that Serena didn't have an answer for. At this point, the only thing she knew that she could do, or could answer, was to try to find a way to counter the power she was feeling. But Arowend, surprisingly, was watching her with a different expression in his eyes.

Is it one of understanding?

"Serena?" Tessatha asked.

"I know it sounds ridiculous," she began, "but I also know that it seems to me that the palace itself was somehow responsible for all of this. It's trying to encourage us to do something, but I don't know what it is. I thought… Well, I suppose it doesn't matter what I thought, as I thought that it was trying to encourage us to find an understanding of our essence, but maybe that's not it at all. The only thing I've learned about my essence is that it's not enough to counter the unity, despite everything I have learned about it. I can't do enough."

"I think you're right," Arowend said.

"You do?" Tessatha asked.

"At least, I think she is right about what the tower wants of us. It wants us to gain a certain understanding of what is happening around us, even if we can't do anything with it. When I was trapped, I felt as if it were trying to concentrate some of that essence down upon me and holding it in a way that seemed as if it were going to collapse that power. But I also recognize that it gave me an opportunity to try to find something more than what I had before."

"What do you mean more?" Serena asked.

They didn't have much time, as the figures were getting closer. Serena was increasingly certain that they were constructs. They radiated a sense of unity.

It wasn't just from the creatures that she felt it. She felt it from the walls, ceiling, and that hazy energy that Arowend had descended through, and she spoke it coursing through her. It seemed to be pressing into her in an almost painful way. She tried to ignore it, trying to make sense of what it was that she was feeling, but even as she attempted to do so, she could not tell whether there was going to be anything that she was going able to do with that power.

"I don't know," Arowend admitted. "All I know is that the kind of power that was there, trapping within me, gave me a sense of energy that seemed to be tightening down, to the point where I had no choice but to explode outward and to try to regain some semblance of my form."

"What kind of form are we talking about?" Tessatha asked.

Arowend turned to her, and there was a bit of a smile on his face. "This one. The Netheral, as well. I felt like I was breaking free. And I know how this sounds, but I felt as if I were finding my way again. I have felt so lost for a long time. And it wasn't until you came around that I feel as if I have started to find myself and find what I am supposed to do and supposed to be."

Serena smiled, wishing she could feel the same way, but didn't she? It was because of Rob that she felt as if she understood what she was supposed to do, and she felt as if she understood who she was supposed to be. Had he not come around, what would she have been? She would've wandered through his valley, testing power, and trying to find a way to make sense of everything that existed, and yet, she would eventually return home. She never would have gone into the Borderlands, never would've come to understand the Spread, never would've learned about the ice king, and never would've found her father. Would she have ever progressed to what she is now?

No. She wasn't sure that she would have.

She would've been trapped as a dragon mind, nothing more than that, for the remainder of her days, at least until her mother decided to offer her something if she ever would have. And she would have been trapped in that form, never able to become something greater unless her mother perished.

That wasn't anything that Serena wanted. She didn't want to lose her mother simply so that she could advance. It felt wrong and as if she were being selfish if that was what she wanted.

She felt like Rob. They all needed and wanted to progress together, all of them needing and wanting to find a way to draw power up so that they could become something more.

"I'd like to take on a form like you," Tessatha said.

Serena had started to push outward, using a combination of her types of essences, creating nothing more than a barrier that the other entities at bay. She didn't know if it was going to work very long, as she could feel that power continued to press toward her, and squeezing on her, but she also recognized that if she didn't do this, they might not have the time they needed.

"It's going to be dangerous," Arowend said.

"I know."

"What are you talking about?" Serena asked.

"She's talking about finding a way to reach dragon form," he said.

"No," Tessatha said. "I'm talking about finding a way to *become* the essence."

"That is far too dangerous. It involves losing yourself. It involves—"

"I know what it means," Tessatha said. "It means that I might become like him. It means I can be *with* him."

"You don't have to sacrifice everything to be with me," Arowend said. "We can be together without you abandoning everything that you aren't everything you can be."

Serena smiled at that. "Why don't we talk about this after? We have a little bit of an issue coming up here. Until we deal with it, I'm not sure it makes sense for us to be talking about the two of you and whatever romantic venture you want to engage in."

And as weird as it was for her to think about, it did sound romantic. They were talking about finding a way to be together, finding some way that they could experience the world in the same manner. Wasn't that what she and Rob wanted?

But then, unless she had some way of reaching unity, she wasn't sure that she was even going to be able to have that with Rob. She wanted more, but she knew that she did not have it, and she increasingly began to wonder if she could have it.

She needed unity.

The essence was within her, blended together, getting her the opportunity to continue to push out and try to counter anything that was there, but even as she focused on what she could feel, she was not able to detect anything more than what she already had.

Other than the essence that was battering down upon her.

Then the barrier she had created broke.

Arowend seemed to recognize that it broke the moment that it did, and he lost his form, transitioning from what he was into something else. He turned into this hazy sort of energy, and he blasted free, streaking away. Once he did, she felt the power circling around these different essence entities.

"It's not going to work," Serena said. "When I was holding them back, I could feel that it wasn't going to work. They're too strong, and we do not have enough."

"I don't think he's trying to destroy them," Tessatha said.

And Serena started to watch, trying to make sense of what Arowend was doing. But as Serena noticed, she was right. Arowend wasn't attempting to destroy anything. Instead, all he was doing was circling around them. And then he slammed into the nearest of the essence entities. When he did, essence met essence. He was a nebulous cloud of power. But he was not unity essence.

And for a moment, Serena thought it wasn't going to work. Arowend was little more than a cloud, little more than an energy, and little more than the wrong kind of power that wasn't going to work.

But then she noticed something else. She noticed that power was beginning to swirl and swell, and she noticed that he began to work his way through the nearest of the constructs.

That was all the time that she had.

The other constructs came toward them.

They were not well formed. Not at all like Arowend had used when he had been the Netheral, creating distinct constructs that had created distinct dangers for them. This was almost indistinct. She focused on what she could see, and then she darted forward. Serena used a blast of fire, burning through the construct, and followed it with ice that crackled, creating a surge of energy that washed over the nearest of the constructs.

As it did, it began to crackle, the flames sweeping over it. Then it started to change, some part of it shifting, as the construct began to lose some of its forms. Serena was watching for a moment until she slammed life essence at it. Rob had been the one to teach her that life essence could devour, and she used that opportunity to try to sweep life essence through it, hoping that it might consume what was there. She didn't know if it was going to work, as she could feel some part of that life essence starting to take hold, but it was definitely a part of what was there. It started to swirl, and then...

Then unity began to expand. It was potent, far more potent than what Serena could counter. But did she have to try to counter it?

Maybe what she needed to do instead was not to counter it, and instead try to find a way of *using* her power, letting it flow out from her, and hopefully building in a way that she could then draw outward, and perhaps even do something similar to what Arowend was doing. He was disrupting the essence, not trying to destroy it. And maybe that was all she needed to do. Disrupt.

She hadn't attempted to do anything like that before, but it made sense to her. Disruption would be straightforward, and it wouldn't be as destructive as what she had been trying.

"Do you think we can do anything like that?" she asked Tessatha.

"I think that we are going to be able to do anything quite like Arowend, but we may be able to help," she said.

Arowend was shifting, swirling, and sending power out through him in a way different from what she could do. And yet, even as she was attempting to follow what he was doing, she realized that what she needed wasn't to destroy. She thought that she could not even destroy it. The unity would not permit it.

She slammed essence into these constructs, and rather than trying to tear it apart or consume it with life, all she wanted was to unsettle what the construct around her attempted to do.

She used a series of different attacks, sending one after another toward them as she battered at them, trying just to disrupt the essence within them. It was not as effective with her singular essence. She noticed that Tessatha was doing something a little different, combining her essence as she was beginning to blast at them, disrupting the power there.

Finally, Serena found that she had gotten through one of them. The disruption was not what she expected. As she pushed on her essence, she pressed through the figure...

And surprisingly felt a connection to it.

It reminded her somewhat of how she felt the connection to the librarian and the soldiers within the palace. It was almost as if there was a link that had formed, but it wasn't a link so much as it was an understanding.

The figure reacted to her thought. She commanded it to stop. And it stopped.

She looked over to shape. "Link to them," she said hurriedly. "I can't tell what's happening here, but as I link to it, it is reacting to me."

Tessatha frowned, but she nodded and quickly began to add her essence, doing something similar to what she truly had done. The second figure stopped moving.

They are not linking to each other, though. That hadn't been effective, and it seemed to her that the palace had wanted her not to do with that. Instead of linking to Tessatha or Arowend, she instead linked to the tower. At least, to the manifestation of the essence of the tower had been created.

Arowend came to land in the middle of the circle, surrounded by these figures.

"What is it?" Tessatha asked.

"This is what happened to me. This was what I remembered. They surrounded me. All of them had. Then they use that to disrupt everything, shatter everything, and tear it free of me."

"They aren't here," Tessatha said.

Serena tried stepping forward, but the figures stepped closer.

The unity began to compress.

It circled around her, coming from these manifestations, which meant that it was coming from the tower itself. It was as if the tower were trying to destroy her. Crushing her. She could feel it. She could feel the way the tower was trying to build that energy, sending something swirling through her, trying to use its power against her—and against Tessatha and Arowend.

"Not again," Arowend cried out.

"It's going to be all right," Tessatha said, taking Arowend's arm.

He stayed in his physical form. Given the power of the unity that was pressing on them, she wondered if he might not even be able to leave his form. Maybe this was all he could do.

Much like Arowend was saying, it tried to tear some part of her way.

Her essence would end up ripped apart.

That was what Arowend had experienced before when he'd become the Netheral.

She tried to reach through the conduit, trying to

reach for Rob, but she couldn't feel anything. There was an emptiness where she knew there should be some sort of power. He'd blocked her.

Tessatha cried out.

Arowend took her hands. She could feel the power linking between the two of them as if Arowend were trying to hold her together.

But Serena didn't have anybody doing that for her. She didn't have any essence that was here, nothing that would be able to be used to help keep her together, to bridge her, to build that power inside of her. The only thing she had was pain.

She tried to reach for the individual essence, but when she did, she could not feel anything more. They were there within her, but they were not present the way that they needed to be. She tried to call upon that power, but it didn't work.

Serena reached for the others, connecting to them, using her dragon mind ability.

She felt anguish. The pain. She felt Arowend's fear of having the same thing happen to him that had happened before. But he did not fight, would not cry out, and did not do anything other than try to reassure Tessatha.

This was not the Netheral.

Serena had known that he had changed but felt it was another thing altogether.

Serena pushed through the dragon mind connection. She wanted to help them.

"We have to fight," Arowend said.

"I don't think that we do," Serena said. "This power,

whatever it is, I think it's trying to help. Look at them. They aren't attacking. It's just power."

The power was there, just at the outskirts of her awareness.

As in the tests before.

Serena allowed herself to open up to it. She no longer fought. Fighting wasn't going to work, anyway. Instead, she simply accepted it.

She let the unity flow through her. It was powerful. It was painful.

And it stripped away everything that she knew.

Chapter Twenty-Three
ROB

Rob could feel the energy around him beginning to shift and wasn't sure if what he was detecting was related to the power that was there. With every passing moment, the energy around him changed. He could feel what Alyssa could feel. He could feel the way that she was drawing upon power.

The unity.

The others around him looked down toward the nexus, watching it.

They didn't have much time.

Rob sent a connection to Alyssa, sharing with her what he was doing, and then he warned her. She needed to know that he was not leaving her behind, only departing to offer a measure of protection from the subheralds while the others standing around the outside of that essence well allowed their power to flow.

It was working.

He withdrew to his physical body.

As soon as he did, he felt it crackling of energy out and around him and realized that the subheralds had the land surrounding. It was reminiscent of what he had felt when they had targeted him. They ringed the entirety of it, though.

He didn't have enough power to fight his way through here.

"I need you to work quickly," he said to Alyssa.

Power was building. And whatever the subheralds were doing, it was starting to press downward. If he failed here, the land, and Alyssa's realm, would fail.

Rob was the reason they were here, the reason they were still trying to fight, and he was not going to be the reason they lost everything they had gained.

Power washed around him.

There was a wave of it. It rippled. At first, he thought that maybe the subheralds had done something to this land, but then he recognized that wasn't it at all. He could feel the shifting of power here, and he could feel the way that it was drawing outward.

It wasn't the subheralds at all. This was Alyssa.

Alyssa's power continued to wash outward. It worked in rippling waves, one after another, as some part of this realm continued to shift, changing as that power built.

Then the essence was met by another power.

Rob blasted outward and began to focus on the essence within him to give Alyssa and the others time to return.

He was met by one of the subheralds. He could feel the linked connection between the subherald and the others. Rob focused on a beam of his unity essence and harnessed it down into a tight blade, and he slammed into the creature but failed.

This amount of essence should be strong enough, as Rob had used it plenty of times before and thought it could carve through the subheralds, but out here, without his connection to the unity, Rob found it increasingly difficult to manage. He attempted another burst of unity, thinking he could send a blade outward, but once again, it was deflected.

Several of the other subheralds broke off to surround him.

They were horrifying creatures. Massive wings, strange arms and legs, and an unusual beak. He radiated out with a blast of unity essence but could feel the energy draining from him. They were siphoning his essence.

It had to be the same thing they had done to this land.

He lashed out, drawing from the last of the strength of his realm, and he used thin needles of the essence. That power slammed into each of the subheralds. The beam slammed into them, and the creatures dropped.

That left three.

They circled around Rob. He wasn't strong enough with essence to fight that way.

So, he punched one of the subheralds.

He was dragon skin, after all. When he struck the creature, it tumbled, only for a moment, but then it righted itself.

Then a blast of energy struck it.

Unity, but not the kind of unity that Rob used.

Alyssa streaked toward him. She glowed with more

power than he had seen from her before. There was no sign of her miniaturized realm, not as it had been before, and he suspected that she no longer needed it.

She turned to the other subherald. With another burst, she blasted at it with another bold of unity essence. The subherald retreated.

"It worked," Rob said.

"I don't know how," she said, looking around her, her gaze taking in the realm below her.

The others gathered around her. Rob couldn't tell if they had any power within them, certainly nothing strong enough that it would rival what Alyssa now had, but he did detect a change in them.

It came from unity. Their land had shifted, becoming stronger because they had blended their powers and because they had allowed that power to return to what it needed. Did they even recognize what they had done?

And even if they didn't, did it matter?

"I need to draw some of them back," he finally said. "You should be able to erect a border around your realm. It should work to hold onto the subheralds, but even if it doesn't, I can draw some of them away, and then it should give us a chance to fight them more effectively."

"And then what? You help us find a greater power, but I can't help but wonder if now it's tied to this realm and trapped here." She pulled up on the unity.

Rob could feel it coming from her, the power that was flowing within her, and he could feel the energy that she possessed. How could she not want that? But then again, Rob understood what she had been through, and he understood that she had suffered, and her people had suffered, for so long that they did not understand what it might be like for them to try to have real power without having to fear another trying to drain it from him.

But he could try to give them time.

He wanted to help them understand the defenses he had used, and what it might take to deal with the subheralds and the heralds, though Rob didn't know if they had enough time as power started to press inward again.

Alyssa erected more of a boundary, raising her hands, and spreading them. The boundary started to sweep out from her, rising around her realm. It forced the subherald back.

"How am I able to do this?" she asked him.

"I don't know. It's tied to your connection to the realm. But..." He frowned, as he was trying to wonder if there was anything more that they might be able to do, anything more than they'd able to link, but he wasn't sure if that was even going to be possible. And yet, that was the hope, wasn't it?

All along, Rob had been drawing upon the different combinations of powers. He had continued to expand his realm and find a way to become more; this time, he had not become anything more but had helped others. If Rob were able to find a way to help her more, maybe he, and his realm, could become more as well.

"I'm going to return to my land, and I want you to be ready here. Hopefully, we can find a new way to connect."

Alyssa started to say something but turned, looking off into the distance. "You had better be quick, though. If I'm not mistaken, we have three heralds coming."

Rob's stomach dropped. Facing the Eternal had been hard enough.

And now they had three?

He and Alyssa weren't going to be enough for that. He might be able to handle a single herald, if he were able to get back to his land. Three of them were more than what he thought they would be able to handle.

Alyssa didn't have that many allies here. A dozen or so of them, and a dozen that were there to try to rebuild this realm and make it into what it had been before. That wasn't enough.

But maybe it didn't have to be enough.

If Rob was able to find a way to link, and if they were able to connect, then maybe it didn't even matter. But first, he had to get out of there.

He locked eyes with Alyssa for a moment, shared with her what he planned, and then used every bit of his essence to blast forward.

Chapter Twenty-Four

SERENA

SERENA WASN'T SURE WHAT SHE SHOULD DO. SHE COULD feel the power coming out of her and some part of the tower that had changed her. It seemed as if it were bearing down upon her, washing away everything that she had been, but it was doing more than that. It was changing her essence, and blending it, mixing what had once been individual powers into a singular one. She had been connected to that unity enough times, at least with a linked essence, that she thought she could make sense of it until she felt this.

She opened her eyes. She was still inside the tower, but the tower was different. She felt as if she were inside a darkened space, as that had been where she had been before, but it was the sun shining down on her.

"We're at the top?" Tessatha said.

Serena looked over at her and realized that something had changed. She was more substantial, in some way. Then again, Tessatha had always been substantial, but it was something about what she felt from the other woman, the way that she felt the essence within her, that felt more substantial than it had been before. Serena tried to make sense of it, but she couldn't tell whether it was her imagination or not.

"I think so," Serena said.

Where was Arowend? She looked around, as when she had last seen Arowend, he had been holding onto Tessatha's hands.

Now he was gone. Had something happened to him?

Unity was all around her. Unity flowed from the tower, into her, and unity connected her to something that she had not felt for quite some time.

Rob.

And Rob needed her.

"We need to go," she said.

"But I'm trying to make sense of what happened here," Tessatha said.

Serena nodded. "I know, I think that we both need to understand, but at this point, I'm not sure that it's going to be enough. Rob needs us. Can you feel him?"

She closed her eyes for a moment, and when she opened them, she looked at Serena and didn't even need to nod. It was almost as if the essence was directed out of her, and Serena could see what she was trying to tell her. There was so much of this essence that was so different than it had been before. Serena wished she had time to think about it, make sense of her feelings, and comprehend the energy she detected, but she simply did not have that time. It was almost overwhelming for her.

Almost.

Rob was out there. She had not felt him for quite some time. The separation, and that essence, had made it so that she had not been able to know what he needed, but now Serena could feel some part of Rob. Though he hadn't changed, she felt as if he were diminished.

With a burst of essence through her conduit, she sent power through him.

She wasn't even sure if she knew how to do that, but it seemed to come from the tower, as if it were concentrating things, guiding her. There was a bit of confusion for a moment, and she felt Rob's mind linking to hers.

"What happened?" Rob asked her.

"It's a long story, but if I'm not mistaken, Tessatha and myself progressed. Maybe Arowend, but I don't know what happened to him."

"You progressed?"

"Why?"

"I need you."

An image formed in her mind, and she saw horrifying creatures with wings that were attacking him, and there was something that seemed to be following him. Chasing him.

"What is that?"

"Heralds," he said. "I was helping Alyssa and her people find a way to progress. They have their own realm, their own unity. As far as I can tell, Alyssa was able to progress, but she's trying to fight off the other heralds, but I don't know if there's going to be enough time. I need help."

"We will be there," she said.

And for the first time in a while, Serena felt as if she

were on a level playing field with Rob. They both had the same essence and access to unity now. Though he might have come across his essence in a different way than she had, she felt as if she could finally fight alongside him. She was not less than him, not how she had been for so long.

"I'm going," she said to Tessatha. "And I think Rob needs us, but I need you to find Arowend."

"Arowend has already left," Tessatha said. "I think… Well, as far as I've been able to tell from what he's been able to tell me, he recognized it. Rob had a need the moment that the tower released us. And he disappeared."

"He *disappeared?*"

"Arowend's progression is different than ours," Tessatha said as if it were the most obvious thing in the world. "And the way he had power, the way that he's able to connect to it now, is quite a bit different than ours. I'm hopeful we can understand it later, but for now, I think we need to try to help support him as much as we can."

Serena snorted. "Of course, we will support him as much as we can; I'm just surprised he disappeared. I thought he would've stayed with you."

"He must've known I didn't need it," Tessatha said, her voice soft, and then she looked up to the sky. "Are you ready?"

Serena nodded. With a burst of the essence, they took to the air.

Serena could feel the power shifting, and she could feel something different about her. When she had traveled this way before, she had felt a bit of resistance, but she also knew there was a piece to such things. It wasn't as if she had gone slowly; with each level she had progressed to, she had certainly not gone slowly, but now…

Now it felt as if there was something more powerful and quite different than what she had ever experienced. Before she even knew it, she was at the edge of their realm. She had traveled over the water, over the essence that extended out there, the unity continuing to spread even into the water in such a way that Serena found amazing. Maybe Rob did, as well, though he never spoke of it.

But then she saw something. There was the boundary. Now that she was up close to it and was the power the way she was, she could feel that boundary in a way that she had not noticed before, but she also saw the strange creatures targeting Rob.

She looked over to Tessatha, who had traveled alongside her, and was traveling quickly, both streaking toward Rob. By the time they reached the boundary's edge, Rob had nearly reached them.

But he wasn't there yet—and a half dozen of those strange, horrific creatures had surrounded him.

"What do we do?" she asked him.

"Come through," he said.

"I don't know if we can. What happens to our essence?"

An image formed again and was quick, stunted, and dangerous.

It looked to be some way of holding onto essence, of storing and trapping it, but at the same time, she wasn't sure if it was going to be enough. But how could it not be? He wasn't asking her to go very far, just beyond the border.

She funneled more power through to him, using the conduit to gift him even more of the energy she could, and he sent out a series of sharp bolts of unity essence through her and away from her, until they blasted into those horrific creatures. One of them fell. The others seemed to wrap their wings around them briefly enough that they were able to deflect that essence, and he went shooting toward the boundary, shooting upward, or downward, falling harmlessly.

And through it all, Serena was aware of some other power that was building, coming closer and closer to them, to the point where she wasn't even sure if she'd be able to withstand that power, only knowing that she wanted nothing more than to try to counter it. It was powerful in a way that she had never felt before.

Heralds.

That was what Rob had said. That meant that there was more than one coming in their direction. More than one of the heralds. More than one like the Eternal.

A power that was more than what Rob could handle.

Could she and Tessatha do anything?

And she wondered if it would even make a difference.

Then she saw a shimmering of essence around Rob. It swirled, and then it manifested, appearing as Arowend for a moment. His essence was darker than before, but it was also stronger. Serena marveled at just how much power Arowend was able to summon. He streaked through one of the creatures, ripping through it in a way she had never seen Arowend doing.

That wasn't quite right. Arowend had done something similar when they had been inside the tower, using his essence to disrupt. He had swept through this creature, and when he was done, there was no essence remaining in that creature.

It plummeted, landing in the water with a splash.

Not dead, just... weakened.

"Perhaps you stay in our realm," Rob said through the conduit. "Be ready."

She looked over to Tessatha, who remained at the border with her.

Arowend took care of three of the creatures, while Rob took care of the other one. Arowend, in this form, was so much more powerful than he had been before. Joining with that power had changed so much for him that he was and how far more capable than he had ever been before. Serena couldn't help but marvel at how much energy he was able to summon and couldn't help but marvel at just what he was able to do, the way that he was able to strip through the essence and shred these powers away.

Would he be able to do that with one of the heralds?

Once the threat was over, Rob joined her, as did Arowend, at the border.

He took a deep breath, and she could feel the essence funneling into him. She hadn't noticed just how weak he was, but now she could. He was drawing upon essence to recover, his eyes pained.

"Thank you," he said, looking at all of them. "I

would love to hear your story as soon as all of this is over, as I can tell that something impressive happened."

"Oh, just a difficult journey through the tower," Serena said, "as it tested us until we were smart enough to realize that all it wanted to do was to help us progress."

Rob frowned, and then a hint of a smile pulled at his lips. "That's… a lot."

"Too much?" Serena asked.

"No. But I wonder if you are now connected to the tower the same way you had been connected to your palace. And if so, I don't know what that means for progression."

"I think everybody has a different way of progressing," Tessatha said. "There is your way, and then there are the ways others might be able to do it. It seems like you're leading us toward something dangerous," Tessatha said. "But I don't know what."

"I don't either," Rob said. "I've been trying to help these others."

An image flashed in her mind, and from how Tessatha looked and Arowend, she suspected that the same image came into their minds, of Alyssa and the others, all drawing power. But it was a different kind of power. Serena could tell that there was something foreign to it, the way that they were accessing it seemed to be quite a bit different than what they had done before. She felt it, even if she wasn't entirely sure what it was.

"Another nexus," Arowend said.

Rob looked over. "Another, and they found their own unity, but it's different than ours. More than ever, I start to think that unity is going to be the key. I'm not sure how, but if we can find a way of connecting to them…"

Rob didn't have a chance to finish, as a burst of power slammed into the barrier. It caused the barrier to shimmer.

"That wasn't subherald power," Rob said.

"Subherald?"

Rob nodded. "Those are the creatures. They are the subheralds. There are many of them, and they are powerful. And as far as I been able to tell, they serve the heralds."

"So it wasn't a subherald power, then it means—"

"The heralds are here," Rob said.

Serena looked out. She couldn't see anything but could feel the power out there.

Rob hovered and sent out a call. It was faint, but she heard it. And she realized why it was faint. It wasn't meant for her. He was sending out a message to all the others inside of the realm. He needed help.

"Join us at the boundary," Rob said. "Those of you who have power. Those of you who have progressed. Dragon soul or higher," he said.

"Higher?" Arowend asked, looking at him.

"There have to be more than just dragon souls," Rob said. "Anybody lower than dragon soul might not be able to do much here. But out here…"

"Out here is beyond the borders of the realms," Serena said.

"Beyond the borders of our traditional realms," Rob said. "But now the realm has been blended. You can feel it. I can."

Serena closed her eyes, and at that moment, she could feel that energy. She could feel the way the essence was blurred, blending, and she could feel what it was doing. She noticed how that power had swept through, giving others, she suspected, the ability to use the same kind of essence. They needed not just unity but the aspect of unity. It made it so that they didn't have to depend upon one realm or another for them to have power. It would mean the dragon souls didn't have to be confined to one space.

And gradually, far too gradually, she felt power coming.

Would it be in time?

From the grim look in Rob's eyes, she knew they needed something to happen quickly. Even then, it might not be enough. Maybe *they* wouldn't be enough.

Another blast of energy struck the barricade.

When it did, the barricade rippled again for a moment, and then it fell still.

Finally, the barricade fell.

And swarms of power came toward them.

Chapter Twenty-Five
ROB

Rob was thankful that he was back in his realm. It was amazing seeing what Arowend had been able to do. His use of essence, at least in this form, had been nothing short of amazing. He had always known that Arowend was incredibly powerful, but he hadn't seen him using his essence quite like this before. Now that he did, he couldn't help but feel as if maybe Arowend was going to be the key to whatever they were doing. But maybe it wasn't just Arowend, but Arowend demonstrating the power of essence in this unstructured fashion. Using that and having an opportunity to do something similar to that, might give them a chance to do had to be more. Rob wasn't sure what that might be, but he had a sense that if he could figure it out, and find a way of doing it, they might be able to overpower what had happened to them.

Then the barricade fell.

When it did, it was almost as if it were a pain to him.

Rob recognized that power recognized the way it dropped and that some part of it made it difficult for him to do much of anything else. Rob tried to be ready for more, but he couldn't tell what else he was going to be able to do. That power was too much for him.

Then he saw shimmering coming through. It was subtle, but it was obvious to him, given that he had this connection to the essence that he did. He could see how they were starting to streak through the barricade, that power that was cascading in, trying to get past, until they managed to succeed. Rob fought, using the only thing he thought he could do, and began to send a sweep of essence upward.

In this realm, connected as he was, he found it easier to do than it had been before, but still not easy. There was too much pain in what he had been doing before.

Then he felt the effect of the heralds.

They were blasting at him. Rob could feel that energy sweeping at him, power that pounded upon them. Three heralds. That was what Alyssa had said. Would they be able to withstand three heralds?

Rob had no idea whether they would. Having four of them who had progressed to its unity essence, five including Alyssa, might be enough, but there were only four of them here. It depended upon how many of the heralds targeted his realm, and how many of them targeted Alyssa.

But why would they come here if they could take care of Alyssa first, and then come? Take off one at a time, and then target him. That seemed to be the smart strategy, as far as Rob could tell.

Maybe there was something that he would be able to do.

"I need your help," he said to Alyssa.

"I'm a little bit busy here," she said through the connection. "I have several dozen of the subheralds still attacking, and I've been trying to counter them, but they continue to appear. I've never seen so many at one time, and though I now have more essence than I ever did before, I can't help but feel as if we are going to be strong enough. And that's not to say anything about the heralds that still might appear."

"But the heralds aren't there, are they?"

"Not yet, but—"

"I think the heralds are going to come to my realm, and I'm going to need you to help me. We need to link our lands."

"What do you mean *link* our lands?"

"I've been thinking about it for a while, and I've been trying to make sense of what it is for us to be able to do, but I wasn't sure if it would make sense for it to work. But increasingly, I think that the real strength here, and maybe the real progression here, is for us to find a way to bridge our two lands. You have unity, I have unity, and though it might be different, it must be similar enough that we can use some aspect of it to try to overpower some of this."

He looked around. Tessatha was fighting with three subheralds. The Netheral—or Arowend, though it was difficult to tell given that he would fade into his hazy form—slammed through five of them, sweeping past them, and ripping essence out of them. Serena was handling it, but even that might be too much for her. But that didn't even matter. She didn't have to do it on her own. More and more of his people began to appear, more and more coming to join, adding their own essence, adding to the fight. There were other creatures of power that were fighting beyond the subheralds, other creatures that his people needed to counter. And there were quite a few dragon souls now, some dragon blood, though not as many as he had hoped, and there was still Maggie, joining in and manifesting. But she manifested with such strength, that Rob couldn't help but wonder if perhaps she was actually here.

All of this was working. They were defending themselves.

Then he felt another shimmering of power.

It came from above, below, and it came from someplace deep.

Heralds.

"The heralds are here," he said, sending it through to Alyssa.

"Good luck," she said.

"I need you to find some way of helping me link the unity. I don't know what it's going to take, but I can tell you that it must be the key."

More and more, Rob couldn't help but feel as if that was what they needed to do. If he could find some way of linking them, some way of drawing upon that power, some way of finding the unity, then there had to be something more that he be able to do. Rob didn't know what it was going to be comedy didn't know what was going to look like, but he couldn't help but feel as if that answer was there. It struck him as something significant, something profound, but it struck him as if there had to be some aspect he might be able to find.

Yet, he could not tell what it was even as he struggled with it.

The heralds started their attack.

Rob could feel the energy. He had built the barricade and tried to redirect it, but even as he attempted to do so, he wasn't able to succeed. He could feel that power rising around him, the power that was working within him, a power that seemed to be trying to offer him some aspect, some memory, but even as he attempted to do so, he couldn't feel anything more.

But he also didn't want to take the time to do so. He wanted to try to hold off, to try to see if there was going to be something that he might be able to use, but even as he attempted to do so, Rob could not feel any aspect of it. He tried to draw upon that power and make sense of it, but when he did, he could feel some part of it pushing against him.

And that power was difficult for him to counter. Rob tried to use what he had access to, but the heralds were too strong.

He focused on Tessatha, Arowend and Serena and tried to link to them. The combination of the four might be enough to grant him more power, as he had always known that linking power was the key to so much, but in this case, it didn't seem as if it were doing anything. He attempted to solidify that link, but when he did…

When he did, he could feel the pressure still pushing against him, and it faded.

The heralds were stronger than the Eternal.

They progressed.

There was no other way to describe it other than that, as Rob could not do anything against them. That power was building in a way that Rob could not counter, building in a way that was rising around him, and building so much that the only thing that he thought that he might do to stop it would be to continue to fight.

"Something is changing here," Alyssa said.

"What is it?"

"I can see it. Let me show you."

An image formed, and he saw a tower.

He smiled. "Connect to it."

"What do you mean *connect* to it?"

"You need to connect to it, and I'm going to have you connect to Serena."

He bridged the two of them and shared with her what he needed to do. Given that Rob was connected to both of them, he could feel it when Alyssa did whatever she could do with her tower and felt the way Serena did what she could do, and then he had to be the one to link it.

He knew that, somehow. He had no idea what it was going to take, and no idea whether it was going to make a difference, but the only thing that he could feel, the only way that he could feel it, was the power that was within him.

He needed to link the two powers.

Rob felt for the energy within Serena. It was there. Power battered down upon him, the power that he was trying to counter with his own unity essence, but the heralds were strong. He could not even see the heralds but could feel what they were doing. They had some way of making themselves invisible to him. But then there was something else. He felt Alyssa. He felt the connection that she had. And Rob realized it wasn't so much about opening the conduit to them but drawing it through himself.

He had to be the unity.

He started to build that power through him. It was potent.

And it was surprisingly familiar.

The unity from his realm was obvious and easy, but how Serena connected to it was quite different from what Rob had. It felt pure in a way that he had not known before. And he understood why. It felt as if all the essence had been purified, concentrated down, and becoming something more than what it had been before. He recognized that power and the way it was rising, but he also knew that there was some other aspect that he was going to have to draw upon, some aspect that Rob did not have control over.

Then he shifted to what he could feel of Alyssa.

Her essence was unique, as well. But it was no less pure. Rob had known that instinctively and had known that she was going to be able to have some way of commanding power, drawing upon energy and essence that would allow them to do what they had not been able to do before. He felt the purity within her, the connection to her unity, and he felt the way he could bring them together, through him.

And as he started, he realized that maybe he wasn't even the right person to do this.

"Arowend," he said, his voice calling out.

Arowend shimmered for a moment, and then he appeared before him. He was fluctuating in and out, manifesting, then turning into the cloud of essence that he was. And the way they did, the rapidity to how he managed to fight, was unlike what Rob had seen before.

"I need you. I need your unique form of essence."

"What do you mean by my unique form?"

Rob was holding onto the link to power. He could feel how that energy buzz within him. It wasn't the same way that he had felt before, and he wondered if there would be any way for him to bridge one unity to the next, and he questioned if that would even be possible. If it was, it might make them stronger. Not only that, but it might give him access to power that he hadn't had before. He had to find some way to hold onto it and to link it truly.

But that wasn't how he was going to handle the heralds.

That was going to be on Arowend.

"You are the essence. I'm going to give you the essence. Pure, raw, and unified essence."

Before short had a chance to answer, Rob focused on the two different forms, and blended them together inside of himself, feeling a burning sort of pain as it happened, before they mingled in him. And then he pushed that out to the connection they shared was Arowend. The other man—essence manifestation? — took that power, and there was a burst within him. It was almost as if some part of him exploded with more power than Rob had ever seen from him before. That essence glowed inside him, then he looked at Rob, locked eyes with him, and departed.

Rob didn't even watch. He could feel what Arowend was doing. He felt it when he reached the first of the heralds. Rob couldn't even see the herald, but he could feel them. They were strong, but this unified essence, this link between the two lands, bridged through Rob, and handed to another, was more than what they could counter. The Netheral—and at this point, Rob couldn't help but feel as if it were both Arowend and the Netheral, but when in this form, it was more likely to be the Netheral—slithered through the other. There was resistance. Somehow, Rob was aware of that resistance, and he could feel it fluttering, but then Arowend pushed, sweeping in that essence cloud until it stripped off the power of the herald.

The herald dropped.

Tessatha was there. She gathered them. Suddenly visible, he looked like an old, frail woman, and she wrapped them in essence, bundling them together, and keeping them from going anywhere.

She looked up at Rob, then up to Arowend, and remained in place.

All around, they were still battling. He felt the essence of his people, people of his realm, battling against the strange and powerful essence that attempted to surge past what had once been the barrier. Rob would love to erect another barrier, but at this point, he wasn't even sure if that was the right strategy. Now that he felt this link between, he and Alyssa and the realms, he couldn't help but wonder if what he needed to do was to keep that open, to give them a chance to move between, and to give them a chance to blend everything truly.

Arowend continued to attack.

Rob felt the essence mingling between him, Serena, Tessatha, Arowend, and, most important, Alyssa. That combined essence continued to flow, and it drifted out of them, through Rob, where he had to do more than just bridge it. He had to link one to the other. The longer he held it, the more he could feel the tower in Alyssa's realm. That was odd, but maybe it shouldn't be. The tower was there, that power was there, and it was flowing in a way that Rob could not ignore. He struggled with it, trying to hold onto it, but as he did, he began to feel some part of it pulling.

And he pulled back.

But then he noticed something.

There was a bridging within him.

Somehow, that bridging ignited something within him. He had felt the burning when he first linked the two powers together, but now the power that he felt, the burning that he detected, was quite a bit brighter and more profound than before. He attempted to ignore it, not wanting to be overwhelmed by that power, but he couldn't help but feel as if there was so much of it that surged inside of him, so much of it that mingled, that he could not help but try to fight past.

And he did.

He had to stop fighting, though. That was the message when he felt the unity essence. And it was the message that he felt from Serena. She wanted him to allow that power to flow. She wanted him to let that energy work its way through him, and she wanted him to surrender.

Rob found that easier than he knew that Serena did. He recognized that power, and he recognized what he was able to do; he recognized what he needed to do. Because he had done it so many times before, he had gone to places where the power was beyond him, and he had come out of it stronger. In this case, he allowed himself to surrender to that power, and it burst within him.

He became the link.

The realms bridged.

And then he felt a connection form.

As soon as it did, Rob sent a rippling wave of a barricade outward. No longer did it separate his realm from Alyssa's. No longer was there a need for such a thing? He erected the barricade, separating his realm from that of this other entity, the entity that he did not yet know, but he was determined to understand.

And he trapped the remaining herald inside.

But even that wasn't a concern. As that power fully linked, Arowend was filled with so much power, and it flowed through him so that he continued to sweep through the other two heralds. There was an energy there that had not been there before. And Arowend began to let that power sweep through these others. And it destroyed them. Tessatha was there, as she had been the first time, and she gathered the remaining people, holding them. There was another woman and another man.

They now had four of the heralds. Three of them had been stripped of power.

As the barricade began to form, solidifying around his realm and around Alyssa's, he headed to where Serena watched. The battle began to fade, and the danger passed.

But for how long?

As his barricade formed and Rob could feel that power within him, he recognized something more. Maybe because he had been limited before because his realm had been limited before, he hadn't known about it, but given the link that he now had to Alyssa's damaged realm, Rob felt much more than he had. He felt the pressure. He felt the power. And he felt the overwhelming strength that existed out there. It was the strength that the heralds represented.

He turned to Serena. "Can you feel it?"

"I can't feel anything. I can just tell that you are troubled by something. Whatever it is, we can handle it."

Rob could feel the linked land, and he could feel the power that existed through that. If that was the key to progression, finding unities, linking them together, then he knew what he could do and what he had to do. He wasn't sure that they would be able to do it, though. They had to find more like them.

"I hope so," he said.

"Hope? That's not the Rob that I know."

"Normally, I would say that we need to progress, but

I'm not sure that we are going to be able to progress. I think this other entity is chasing the same thing."

"What do you mean?"

He shook his head. "It's this. These linked unities. This next step is moving beyond, but to do so, we need to have the power of others around us."

"So, what will we have to do?"

"I don't know."

One possibility was that they might have to steal that essence, but that wasn't what Rob wanted to do. He didn't know what he was going to be able to do. He didn't know what he could do. What he knew was that they had to find unity. And they had to link them. And from what he could tell, that was going to be the key to the next stage in progression.

This time, though, they had people to question. The heralds would talk.

And he was determined that they would get their answers.

Don't miss the next book in Blood of the Ancients series: Dragon Form.

An impossible power is coming. None are prepared.

The power the heralds serve has begun to move, swallowing everything in its wake.

As Rob races to save his realm, he realizes the key to stopping it won't be found in his realm at all.

But how can he use unity—and link realms—in places this power has already consumed?

Progression may no longer be possible. And if it's not, how can he save everything he cares for?

Series by Dan Michaelson

Cycle of Dragons

The Alchemist

Blood of the Ancients

Similar Series by D.K. Holmberg

The Dragonwalkers Series
The Dragonwalker
The Dragon Misfits
The Dragon Thief
Cycle of Dragons

Elemental Warrior Series:
Elemental Academy
The Elemental Warrior
The Cloud Warrior Saga
The Endless War

The Dark Ability Series
The Shadow Accords
The Collector Chronicles
The Dark Ability
The Sighted Assassin
The Elder Stones Saga

Printed in Great Britain
by Amazon